A Long Time Coming

Cate Swannell

Yellow Rose Books
by Regal Crest

Nederland, Texas

Copyright © 2012 by Cate Swannell

All rights reserved. No part of this publication may be reproduced, transmitted in any form or by any means, electronic or mechanical, including photocopy, recording, or any information storage and retrieval system, without permission in writing from the publisher. The characters, incidents and dialogue herein are fictional and any resemblance to actual events or persons, living or dead, is purely coincidental.

ISBN 978-1-61929-062-4

First Printing 2012

9 8 7 6 5 4 3 2 1

Cover design by Donna Pawlowski

Published by:

Regal Crest Enterprises, LLC
3520 Avenue H
Nederland, Texas 77627

Find us on the World Wide Web at
http://www.regalcrest.biz

Printed in the United States of America

Acknowledgements:

Thanks to Lori L Lake and Patty Cronin from Regal Crest for their patience, persistence and editing skills.

To Sue. For patience, tolerance, and sense of humour.

Chapter One

Brisbane, Australia
Present day

SHELBY GLANCED DOWN at the stopwatch that rested on the slanted surface of her stage manager's desk. One look at the glowing digital figures told her it was time to get the show on the road. She reached for the phone on the wall above the desk and keyed the switch to broadcast her voice to the orchestra pit, dressing rooms and the green room backstage.

"Five minutes, ladies and gentlemen. Five minutes to curtain. Men's and women's chorus, Mr. Browning, Ms. Fleming, to the stage please."

Shelby replaced the handset and turned back to the stage, giving everything a final visual once-over. Her desk was tucked into the dark front corner, stage left, and although all was quiet onstage, she could hear the constant rumble of the incoming audience. For a few seconds she closed her eyes and imagined the people taking their seats, reading their programs, settling in for their night of entertainment. She stepped out of the darkness and into the dim illumination provided by the working lights. Right now all was tranquil here, the players still backstage, and Shelby wandered to centre stage, her back to the heavy velvet curtain. She heard a brief crackle in her headset.

"Everything all right, boss?" Karen, Shelby's deputy stage manager, asked. She was tucked into her own dark niche on stage right. Shelby peered toward Karen's position and smiled as she keyed the transmit button.

"No problems," she said quietly. "Just checking."

She heard Karen chuckling. "You love this time of the evening, don't you, boss?"

"You know it. We've done everything to get it ready. The actors are happy, the follow-spot operators are hanging from the ceiling, and all's right with my world." Shelby walked back to her desk, smiling at the laughter from the two operators in question as it came through the cans. As she reached her position, the first of the actors moved past her and stepped on to the stage, settling themselves into their places.

The next few minutes passed in silence. Shelby watched the seconds tick by until all the actors were in place. "Dim working lights," she said into her microphone, "and bring up orchestra lights, please. Standby house lights."

"Working and orchestra, house standing by," came the confirmation from the lighting operator. Shelby heard the bells ringing in the foyer, warning the stragglers to get to their seats or risk missing the first half of the show. All went dark around her, except for the glow-worm-like illumination from the orchestra, peeking up from under the bottom edge of the curtain.

"Call it in, folks," Shelby said softly.

"Lighting operator ready."

"Follow-spot one ready."

"Follow-spot two ready."

"Orchestra ready."

"Stage right ready," Karen said, confirming that all the actors were where they should be for the start of the performance. All she needed now was to hear from the front-of-house manager, and that wasn't long coming. "Doors are closed and we're ready."

"Thank you." Shelby opened the first page of her script and smoothed the paper with the flat of her hand. One more glance at the stopwatch, and Shelby took a deep breath. "Lower house lights, standby light cue one."

"House lights out," the LO confirmed, and Shelby saw the darkness descend under the lower edge of the curtain. Almost immediately she heard applause and knew the conductor had stepped into the orchestra pit. Within seconds, the opening strains of the overture began and she let out a long slow breath. If the musicians went at their usual pace, she had about three minutes and forty-five seconds before she needed to cue the next part of the process.

Shelby let her eyes drift to the card pinned to the top of her desk. The front cover was a black and white close-up of a cat's face, a paw brushing lazily forward across its eye. She opened it, re-reading the words that were scrawled in Eve's characteristic hand.

Break a leg tonight. Here's to a long run and a happy show. Love, Eve.

As she had done since opening night a week ago, Shelby frowned slightly as she read the inscription on the inside of the card. Despite living in Eve's back pocket, so to speak, for eighteen months, this was the first time Eve had chosen to mark the opening of one of Shelby's shows in such a personal way.

Not that Shelby was complaining. Not by any means. In fact, it had given her the warmest feeling she'd experienced in a long time. She wished Eve would come to see the show, but so far that hadn't happened.

Shelby cast her mind back to the day she spent with Eve on the couch in front of the big-screen television. After the movies were finished they had kept each other company through a long and leisurely picnic-style dinner. And although they'd had plenty to talk about, neither had chosen to approach the subject of their close encounter earlier in the day.

And since then...Shelby contemplated. Since then we've barely crossed paths. Just too damn busy, the both of us.

"Standby light queue one, standby curtain," she muttered into her headset, the telltale bars of music filtering through her thoughts. Tension rose among the cast as everyone readied themselves. "And...curtain," Shelby directed, waiting a half beat before she ordered the first light cue. A warm glow suffused the stage as the curtain rose, and immediately the heat from the lights washed across the players and into the wings.

"Up and running, boss," came Karen's soft tones.

"Mmhmm. One light cue down, eighty-seven to go," Shelby murmured back.

EVE SETTLED BACK in her seat as the curtain rose.

I probably should have told Shelby I was coming, she thought as she took in the first impression of the set and the actors draped across the stage. I didn't want to disappoint her if I was too tired to come again. I wonder if she'll have time to have a cup of coffee with me afterwards. We need to talk.

Eve felt like she had missed an opportunity when she and Shelby had skirted the issue ten days earlier during their picnic dinner. Her natural instinct, therapist-like, was to let Shelby dictate where the conversation went, and she was now regretting it. Damn, it wasn't a therapy session. I should have talked about what I wanted to talk about. This is a friendship and it's been that way for a long time. Besides, Shelby wasn't going to bring it up. Sixteen years we've known each other and she's still so concerned about offending me.

Eve knew every inch of Shelby's psyche and it didn't surprise her to find Shelby hesitating to press her advantage. After all, that's how it had to be for a long time. That's how I wanted it, needed it to be. Or I couldn't have done what she was paying me to do. And now...Now, I want more. When did that happen?

Refocusing on the stage, she watched the actors moving through the opening scene of the musical. And why would it surprise me that she's hesitating? By all appearances, I've done a 180-degree turnaround about what kind of relationship I want with her, without any explanation.

And as the days had passed since the near-kiss, with little chance to catch up with Shelby, Eve felt the growing need to talk with her.

She glanced toward the wings, wondering where Shelby was stationed. *One day I must ask for a tour backstage. I'd love to know more about what she's doing, what her job is about.* Her attention was drawn back to centre stage and she watched as the lighting changed somewhat as the focus of the action moved. *I guess that's Shelby calling those shots.*

And with that, Eve put further thoughts of her evolving relationship with Shelby to the back of her mind and concentrated on the onstage entertainment.

SHELBY LET OUT a long, slow breath of satisfaction as she watched the highly-rehearsed mechanism that was her stage crew complete the most complicated of the show's set changes. While the biggest pieces of the set were shifted hydraulically by computer-controlled jacks and tracks, there was still plenty for the humans to do in the 15 to 20 seconds afforded them between scenes. The changes were a close-run thing, as they had been every night of the run so far.

Karen made one last quick foray to centre stage before ducking out of sight as the lights came back up. Shelby was gratified to see that the changeover was getting smoother with each performance.

Give us another few shows and we won't remember what we were worried about, she thought.

She noted a palpable sense of relaxation among the crew as the action resumed onstage. Everyone knew it should be a calm cruise to the end of the show now, and chatter between crew members on the cans picked up, both in frivolity and volume. Shelby didn't want to squelch that too much, but she also knew it was easy to lose track of things. And the last thing she needed was the cast bitching about the crew.

"Keep it to the noisy bits, please," she said into her mike, gratified when there was an immediate decrease in output. Shelby hated being a hard-ass and had many happy memories of her own hi-jinks in the wings, but those were in her days as an amateur. These days she was a professional and, what's more, a professional with responsibility.

That didn't stop her grinning when she heard a familiar line of banter in the hushed undertones known as 'wing whisper.'

"Come on, Karen, how about a command performance?" the

senior of the two follow-spot operators, a burly Scotsman called, incongruously, Tiny. "You keep promising me paradise."

Shelby heard Karen sigh dramatically. "Tiny, you know I only do that for special people. I can't do it on cue, y'know."

"That's not what I heard," Ryan, the number two follow-spot operator, said. Shelby lifted an eyebrow. At nineteen he was the youngest member of the crew, and it wasn't like the teenager to pipe up in this kind of exchange.

He must be starting to feel like a part of the team, Shelby thought, pleased.

"Cheeky bastard," Karen said playfully. "I'll have you know my world-famous patented fake orgasm party trick is only rolled out for the privileged few."

"Oh, so we don't qualify?" Tiny asked, and Shelby could almost see the hopeful hangdog look on his red-bearded face.

"Mmmmm, well, I don't know," Karen mused. "What am I going to get out of it?"

Shelby keyed her transmit button and couldn't resist saying, "Doesn't that depend on how fake it is?"

"Boss!" Karen's mock outrage was almost believable.

"Rumor is, you'd know for sure, boss," came Tiny's retort, confirming Shelby's suspicion that the crew believed she and Karen were more than friends.

Ah, well, you can't help bad luck, she decided. "Guess you'll have to let me be the judge, then, won't you, big fella?" A look around one of the black sightscreens showed her Karen's grinning face in the gloom of the wings, stage right. Her deputy stuck her tongue out at Shelby, who chuckled.

"Come on, Karen, you're not going to let that challenge go by, are you?" Tiny asked.

"Rightio, then, I'll give it my best shot," Karen said.

"Wait for the song, please," Shelby pleaded, knowing her entire complement of backstage staff was about to be reduced to gibbering idiots, one way or another.

Three more light cues and then the opening bars of the second act's biggest musical number struck up. Shelby could almost hear the held breath of the four men in the crew. Not to mention the three lesbians.

Once the music was in full swing, Karen started her own performance.

"Ohhh yes," she said, her voice low and husky.

"Bloody hell," came a squeak from someone. Shelby thought it was the usually taciturn lighting operator, Phil.

"Steady, man, it's early days yet," Tiny said, high in the rafters of the theatre.

Karen moaned, and a ripple went down Shelby's spine. "Jesus," she muttered, glad that, of all the crew, only she could choose when to transmit to the rest. A very good thing.

As the song built toward its crescendo, so too did Karen, working her way to a masterpiece of erotic fakery. Shelby felt her palms sweating and could only imagine what the effect was on the rest of the crew.

"Ohhhhh yesssssss, yesssssssss, oohhhhhhhhhhhhhhhhhh."

As applause broke out in the auditorium, Karen panted her way down from her "high" until there was nothing but a pregnant silence in the cans. Shelby was sure she could hear several sets of heavy breathing, and was once again glad nobody was listening to her own respiration.

"Holy Mother of God," came a Scottish-tinged moan from somewhere over the stalls. "You're trying to kill me, aren't you?"

"Hey, you challenged me, Tiny. Ya gets what ya paid for."

"Standby light cues eighty-two and eighty-three," Shelby said, letting the grin that split her face sound in her voice.

"Standing by," came the rasping, desperately heated-sounding response from the LO.

"Oh, and Karen?" Shelby said.

"Yes, boss?"

"Bravissima."

Soft laughter all round.

"So how did it compare to the real thing, boss?" That was Ryan.

Shelby glanced right and again saw Karen grinning at her from the wings. "I never kiss and tell," she said. "Light cue eighty-two, go...and light cue eighty-three...go."

"MS. MACROSSAN?" THE voice in her ear was unfamiliar, but whoever it was had to be connected to the system, so...Shelby keyed her transmit button.

"Right here," she muttered as she packed away a piece of scenery, securing it to its place on the wall with a long octopus strap.

"It's Charlie from the green room reception desk," he said. "There's a lady here says she's a friend of yours and she wants to come in and say hello, but she's not on the list."

Shelby's brow furrowed. "Sure she is. Lynne Wright. I put her on the list this afternoon."

"Oh, no, Ms. Wright is already here and inside," Charlie said. "This is someone else."

"What's the name?" Shelby tossed her gloves on to her desk.

"Ms. Eve Morgan."

Shelby stopped in her tracks. She came. She felt the silly grin widening on her face. How cool is that? A glance around told her there was still work to be done though.

"Charlie, that's Doctor Eve Morgan, and please let the lady in, find her a drink and something to eat. And do me a favor? Let her know that it's probably going to be another twenty minutes or so before I can come out."

"Will do."

Shelby clapped her hands sharply and strode out into centre stage. "Come on, let's get this done."

EVE SAT IN a comfortable armchair, nursing a glass of white wine. It had turned out to be quite a fascinating evening. She had never been in a theatre's green room before and the passing parade of artistes was entertaining in and of itself. Actors mixed with musicians and crew members, who stood out in their all-black outfits. There was also a smattering of what Eve would call "civilians," people who were obviously friends of the company and were sporting the same visitor's badge that she had pinned to her lapel.

Eve's chair was part of a quartet down the left-hand side of the long room. At the far end, and up a level, was a cafeteria, complete with six tables and their accompanying chairs. The lower level was filled with sofas.

"Hello. You looked lonely, so I thought I'd come and keep you company."

Eve looked up to see a rotund, short woman in a diamante-encrusted black evening gown flouncing into the chair opposite her.

"Hello." Eve smiled slightly as the stranger made herself comfortable.

"I couldn't stand up for one more second," the woman said dramatically. "You don't mind do you? Don't be alarmed by me. I'm only half as eccentric as I seem."

"No problem," Eve said. *If you knew what came through my office doors every day you wouldn't even begin to think of yourself as eccentric.*

"Who are you waiting for? I'm Lynne, by the way."

"Eve," she murmured. "Um, a friend of mine is the stage manager."

"Shelby?" Lynne's face lit up. "You're a pal of Shelby's? Me too! Excellent. The more the merrier at the party."

Eve's heart sank a little. Party? Well, of course there's going to be a party, Eve. It's Saturday night and they don't have another show until Tuesday. Of course they're going to party.

"Wait a minute." Lynne was talking again, oblivious to Eve's thought processes. "You're, Eve? 'The' Eve?"

"Um...well, I don't know about 'the' Eve, but yes, that is my name," Eve said, a little bemused by the look of delight on Lynne's face.

"You live with Shelby." She now looked like she was the keeper of the world's biggest secret.

"Uh...more or less." Eve wondered if inhabiting separate floors and never seeing each other actually constituted "living together."

"Oh, I've heard all about you."

Eve decided to ignore that. "And how do you know Shelby?" she asked instead, putting the conversational ball back in Lynne's court.

"Oh, we've known each other for years. I first met Shelby when she crewed for a production of *Mame* I was directing. She was the cutest little baby dyke back then. She must have been barely legal, too. Quite the temptation."

"I was twenty, thank you very much," came a voice from behind them. "And clueless, what's more." Eve watched the arrival of the woman in question. Shelby looked hot and slightly disheveled, but, to Eve's eyes, quite gorgeous in her tight black jeans and black body-hugging sleeveless shirt. Her bare arms were tanned, lean and muscular. Eve found herself staring, a gaze that was met squarely by Shelby's big brown eyes. "Hello, you two. I see you've met." Eve had the impression that Shelby was slightly nervous about that fact.

Lynne bounded up out of her chair with a speed surprising for one so round, and within a second she had Shelby wrapped in a bear hug that squeezed the breath out of her.

"Hello, gorgeous," Lynne bellowed. Eve stood up in her wake and watched, amused as Shelby half-heartedly fought off the attentions of her friend, who managed to plant a wet kiss on her cheek despite Shelby's best efforts to avoid it.

"Hello, Lynne." Shelby caught Eve's eye as she disentangled herself. "Hi," she said softly. "This is a nice surprise."

"Well, I thought it was about time." Eve leaned in and brushed her lips across Shelby's cheek. "It's a good show," she said, blue eyes twinkling.

"Thanks. We had a decent night. The actors managed not to trip over the furniture, and we remembered to put all the props in the right place. You can't ask for much more than that."

Eve was aware of Lynne watching their exchange avidly off to the side, but any further discussion was pre-empted by the tornado-like arrival of another woman, who barreled into Shelby. She wrapped her right arm over Shelby's shoulder from behind and pulled her close.

"We're done, boss, let's go party hard and party hearty."

Eve raised an eyebrow, amused to see Shelby blush. Truthfully Eve was not totally thrilled by the ambush. Lynne, on the other hand, looked like the cat who'd found the cream, her gossip-hound instincts on full alert, Eve was sure.

"Uh, Karen, this is Eve, my...um...landlady."

Karen lifted her hand from Shelby's breastbone long enough to wave it in greeting at Eve. "Hiya. You coming to the party, too?"

Eve took in the tall brunette's easy familiarity with Shelby. "Oh no, I don't think so, thanks," she said easily. "I just wanted to come back and say hello and congratulations." *And the last thing I want to do is try and compete for her time with a room full of boisterous strangers. Damn it.*

Karen leaned closer and said in Shelby's ear. "Come on, babe, let's get moving. The night is young." She finished the statement by placing a playful, nibbling kiss on the nape of Shelby's neck.

Lynne giggled wildly and Shelby glared at her old friend. With her free hand she dug into her jeans pocket and pulled out her car keys. She handed them to Karen.

"Why don't you load up the gear and I'll see you in the car park in a few minutes," she said, her eyes pleading with Karen to give her a break.

"Sure," Karen said, tossing the keys into the air and catching them again with a flourish. "Nice to meet you, Eve," she said, before turning on her heel and striding away.

"I'll...um...go help," Lynne said, her amusement evident to everyone.

"Sorry about that," Shelby said, once the pair had disappeared.

"Nothing to apologize for," Eve said calmly. She was determined not to show her disappointment at missing time with Shelby. To mask her feelings she took a few seconds to place her wineglass on the coffee table next to her chair before straightening up and facing Shelby again.

Shelby said, "Are you sure you won't change your mind and come to the party?"

"No, thanks. I'm about at the end of my energy and I have reports to write tomorrow. Besides you've got friends who want to spend some time with you, and I think they're much bigger party animals than I am." She smiled at Shelby. I knew I should have told her I was coming.

Shelby sighed. "To be honest, I've about had enough of these people for this week. Maybe I should go home."

"No, go out and have some fun. You've got a couple of days to make up the sleep." Eve reached out and patted Shelby's forearm gently. "I'll catch up with you later in the week."

Shelby nodded. "Well, thanks for coming." She waited until Eve's blue eyes met hers. "It meant a lot."

"My pleasure, honestly. Oh, and by the way..."

"Yes?"

"You know how you thought you and Karen didn't have much chance of being more than friends?"

Eve watched the blush rise on Shelby's face again as she shifted her weight from one foot to the other.

"Um, yeah?"

"I think Karen has other ideas." With a soft laugh Eve patted Shelby's arm again and headed for the exit. "Goodnight," she called out as she left.

Chapter Two

EVE GUNNED THE car once she reached the long stretch of freeway that would take her almost to her doorstep. It was a mild spring night, and she opened the car's sunroof to make the most of the breeze. It was good to have the cool air whistling around her as she pushed up and beyond the speed limit on the unoccupied road. The evening had been a pleasant one, and she was always happy to spend time with Shelby, but it was the end of a long day.

She reached forward and punched the buttons on the car's CD player, dialing up her favorite rock song and upping the volume. If any one of her clients could have seen her at that moment, they would hardly have believed the windswept blonde singing along to Queen and the cool, elegant therapist were one and the same woman.

Just the way I like it, she thought as she swept around the long curve before her exit. Now if I could just figure out what to do about Shelby. She dipped down off the freeway and slowed to a respectable speed as she wound her way through the suburban streets. Maybe I'm wrong to be thinking anything about Shelby. I don't know for sure how I feel, after all. Let alone what I want to do about it. A fleeting memory of Shelby's wide-open gaze, up close and personal, warmed the pit of her belly. Well, maybe I know what I'd like to do about it.

She startled as a cat flew out from beneath a hedgerow, streaking across in front of her and causing her to brake and swerve sharply.

"Goddamnit," she muttered, accelerating away again, heart pounding a mile a minute. The rush of adrenalin petered out and Eve felt a wave of weariness taking its place. Long week, and there's too much to do tomorrow.

She pulled into the driveway of her home and reached for the garage door remote control, activating the mechanism as she rolled forward. Within a couple of minutes she was tossing her keys on the dining room table and greeting Rufus. Eve bent down to pick up the black cat, who immediately settled against her shoulder, head-butting her.

"Hello, you," she said. "Hungry?" His answering purr said it all. Rufus was horribly spoiled, largely because he had perfected the art of wrapping Eve and Shelby around his little paw. He had feed bowls in both parts of the house and made the most of his ability to win sympathy from both his mistresses. As a result he was bordering on tubby. "Come on, then, let's see what we can give you."

The cat had been a nice bonus to having Shelby move in to the small flat under the house two years ago. She and Joe had originally added it on to accommodate Joe's ailing mother, but after her death it was wasted space until Shelby came along.

Eve moved into her spacious kitchen, the cat now draped across her shoulders and around her neck. "Has your mama fed you today, boycat?" There was no answer from Rufus, other than his usual deep purr. "Hop down." She bent down to pour fresh kibble into his bowl. "Spoiled rotten, that's what you are." She knew very well that he was probably wolfing down his fourth or fifth square meal of the day.

"And I'm sure mama will be giving you something when she gets home, too." A thought occurred to her. "Assuming she's not otherwise occupied, of course," she muttered, disturbed by how much she didn't like that possibility. *I really don't want to think about her with Karen, right now. Damn.*

"SO COME ON, tell me all about it."

Shelby looked at Lynne, one eyebrow raised. "Tell you all about what, Lynnie? Current affairs? Sport? Politics?"

They were sitting in a corner of a very crowded living room. One of the leads in the show had agreed to host the party and it appeared to be a full house. Actors, musicians, crew and administrators had taken the drive out into the suburbs and by 3:00 a.m. were well-oiled, happy and loud. Lynne and Shelby were practically yelling at each other to be heard over the dance music.

"Don't play silly buggers with me, Shel," Lynne shouted. "I want to know all the gory details of your love life, and don't step over the good bits."

"I don't have a love life, and you know it," she said. "I'm on sabbatical from love." Shelby took a long swig of her Coke and frowned at Lynne, daring her to continue the line of questioning.

But Lynne was oblivious to that kind of subtlety, especially when she was on a mission to dig up gossip, and doubly so when she had a few Lemon Ruskies under her not inconsiderable belt.

"That's bullshit, Shelby," she said, her words slurring only slightly. "From what I've seen so far tonight, you've got more than one card on the table."

Shelby remembered suddenly what a drag it was to be the

only sober one in a room full of drunks. "What the hell are you talking about, Lynne?" She knew damn well what Lynne was talking about and squirmed in her chair. Oh, shut up.

"Come on, quit holding out on me," Lynne insisted. "Karen over there," she gestured toward the willowy deputy stage manager who was doing a fair impression of Britney Spears in the middle of the room's makeshift dance floor. "Is clearly hot for you, and from what I saw of the lovely Dr. Headshrinker tonight, she's up for it as well. So, come on, what gives?"

A headache sprang from nowhere to reside between Shelby's eyes. She pressed the cold, wet glass of the Coke bottle against her forehead and sincerely wished there was a way she could get out of this conversation.

"Lynne, Karen is sweet and funny and I like her a lot, but there's nothing there that I want to...follow up on."

Lynne looked at her steadily. "I think you're nuts. I mean, look at her." Both women watched as Karen, her long hair flowing behind her, spun around in a wild dance in the middle of the floor. There was no questioning the young woman's beauty and attractive personality. "But sure," Lynne continued dryly. "I can see that there's no appeal there."

"Oh shut up. She's gorgeous and we both know it."

"And like I said, she's hot for you, babe."

"Lynne," Shelby said, in warning.

"What about the good doctor, then?"

Shelby groaned. "You're not going to leave this alone, are you? You're going to be relentless until you get the answer you want, right?"

Lynne's eyes widened. "You got it."

How do I get into conversations like this? I'm not sure I'm ready to even think about this stuff, let alone talk about it with anyone other than Eve. "There's nothing to tell. She's my therapist." What a great excuse.

Lynne laughed so hard Shelby thought she was going to rupture something. "You are so full of it, you know that, right?" Shelby slumped back in her chair, letting her head rest on the back of it, as Lynne continued her argument. "You've been talking to me about this woman for years, and we both know she hasn't been your therapist for...what? Four years, now?"

"Yeah, yeah."

"Yeah, yeah nothing. It matters, Shel. You can't use that as an excuse anymore."

Shelby looked at Lynne. "I'm not using it as an excuse." *Bullshit.* "But it complicates things, you have to admit."

Lynne sighed. "I'm not admitting anything, kid. You want it

to be complicated. Seriously, what's holding you back?"

Shelby regretted telling Lynne about her close encounter with Eve the week before. *I should have known she would blow it out of all proportion and hound me about it.*

"A whole bunch of things," she muttered.

"Like what?"

"I'm not ready for a new relationship." *That at least was the truth.*

"It's been five years, Shel."

Shelby closed her eyes and allowed the well-buried pain to wash through her for a moment. Amanda was the heartbreaker, the one she thought she'd be spending the rest of her life with. And for six years it was perfect. And then it wasn't.

"You know how I felt about her."

"Yes, I do, better than most, probably. Except Eve, of course," Lynne said. "But I don't want to see you alone and miserable any longer."

"I'm not miserable." *And that was also the truth.* She had actually found a great deal of contentment, if not happiness, in her solitary life since the awful year she spent getting over her break-up with Amanda. *And a lot of that is down to Eve.* "I'm also not willing to get into all of that right now. I don't think."

"But you're not sure."

"Right now I'm not sure about anything too much, especially about Eve."

"Ah-hah! So you admit it then!"

Oh good grief. "Admit what?"

"That there is something going on with Eve."

"I'm about to turn 38, not 138. What the hell is the rush?"

Shelby was saved from further circular argument by the sudden arrival of Karen. She landed hard in Shelby's lap and immediately locked lips. The kiss was deep and left little to the imagination. By the time Karen broke the embrace, Shelby was dizzy and lightheaded.

"Hiya, gorgeous," Karen said.

"Hi, there." *Why does she have to taste so good?* Shelby groaned internally, disconcerted by her body's reaction to the kiss.

"Come and dance with me." Karen scrambled out of Shelby's lap and pulled her up. "Time to samba, baby."

Shelby caught Lynne's eye and shrugged helplessly before allowing Karen to drag her into the melee of dancers in the middle of the room.

THE PARTY WAS closer to Shelby's place than Karen's so it had seemed logical to bring Karen back home for a night on the couch, rather than dragging her across town. At least, it seemed logical at the time. With Karen's damn-near dead weight dragging down on Shelby's right shoulder as she pulled her up the driveway toward the front door, Shelby suddenly wasn't so sure anymore.

"Should have poured you into a taxi," she muttered, knowing that her words were wasted on Karen.

"Huh? Wh-wassamatter?" Karen's eyes fluttered open and for a moment she almost seemed capable of taking all her own weight on her feet. "Hey, Shel, how's it goin'?" A dreamy, silly grin gave some much-needed life to Karen's otherwise washed-out face.

"Ssssshhhh, for Christ's sake," Shelby whispered. She was very conscious of the close proximity of Eve's bedroom window one floor up and to the right of Shelby's door.

Last thing I want to do is wake her up.

The light was the murky grey of pre-dawn. Shelby knew Eve would likely be awake soon anyway, but there was something deeply uncomfortable about the thought of her friend seeing Karen following Shelby inside.

Don't really want to think about that right now.

"Aw c'mon Shel, don't be a spoilsport," Karen slurred, pushing herself up and away from Shelby. She spun around in a very wobbly pirouette, her arms waving dangerously close to Shelby's face.

"Oh, come on, Karen, give me a break," Shelby said as she tried to grab hold of the wayward woman.

"Shhhhhh," Karen said in the loudest stage whisper Shelby had ever heard. But then it got worse. "There's a kind of hushhhhhhhhhhhhhhh, ALL over the worrrrrrrrrld, tonight," Karen bellowed. "ALL over the worrrrrrrrld, you can hear the sounds of lovers in LOOOOOOOOOOOOOVE." Karen spun away across the front lawn, narrowly missing Eve's prize azaleas.

"Oh fuck, shoot me now." Shelby groaned.

EVE LAY IN the dark, listening to the sounds of Shelby's struggle with Karen on the front lawn. The truth was she had been only lightly dozing, her sleep disturbed by swirling, frustrating dreams she couldn't pin down. The sound of Shelby's car door slamming had woken her completely.

Eve lay on her back, staring at the ceiling. There was enough illumination to get her bearings, and it was hard to ignore the singing coming from below. Shelby wasn't doing the singing— Eve had heard enough of her friend's warm alto to know that Shelby couldn't sound that bad no matter how drunk she was. No, that was Karen.

Big assumption, Eve. It could be anybody from the party, after all. Then again, I know who my money's on. It felt strange, acknowledging the twinge of jealousy she felt.

The singing stopped and Eve thought she heard more hushed conversation from below her bedroom. Then Shelby's front door slammed. Eve smiled into the gloom, despite her misgivings about Shelby's company.

Whoever it is, it sounds like Shelby's got her hands full.

Eve rolled on to her side and curled up, her hands pillowing her head. She could feel Rufus settling himself against the back of her knees and she enjoyed the warm softness of the boycat. Usually he made a beeline for Shelby's bed, but with her out most nights of the week, he would seek out Eve's company.

Maybe he knows something I don't.

"Tch, get over it," she muttered, before closing her eyes again, determined to get a little more sleep before her Sunday dawned.

"YOU GONNA MAKE me sleep on the couch, Shel?"

Karen was sprawled across the aforementioned piece of furniture, resting back on her elbows while she looked up at Shelby through long lashes.

Jesus. Shelby put her hands on her hips and looked back. It was hard to ignore Karen's beauty, and Shelby had known her long enough to be well-acquainted with the warm personality and sharp intelligence beneath the surface.

She liked Karen. A lot. But right now, the younger woman— *too young for you Shelby-girl*—was a sloppy mess. Cute, but a mess.

"Yep, I am," Shelby said aloud.

"Awww, come on, don't be like that. I promise to be good." Karen grinned in a way that didn't convince Shelby of her sincerity, and held up two fingers. "Scout's honor."

"It's a comfortable couch, Kar. You'll get a great night's sleep on it, I promise."

Karen pouted. "Don't want a good night's sleep. Want to curl up with you."

Well, there ya go, Shelby. If you had any doubts before about what her intentions were, there can't be a lot left. Shelby let out a long, slow breath. She felt a strange sense of pressure at the back of her neck, and she wondered if things were getting a bit too complicated. She was thankful Karen was drunk because it meant she had an excuse for not taking this any further. An excuse that had nothing to do with Eve.

"That's sweet, babe," Shelby said to Karen. "But I make it a rule not to take advantage of the young and intoxicated." She hoped her smile would take the edge off the rejection.

"What about the young and sober?"

Oh, you're drying out with every passing minute aren't you? I'm going to have to keep an eye on you. "Well, we'll talk about it next time you're sober."

"Promise?"

Shelby sighed, not really wanting to think about when that conversation might be. "I promise."

"Cool." And with that, Karen curled into a ball on the couch. Shelby opened the linen cupboard, pulling out a blanket and two pillows. Karen was already asleep, a low snore puffing out her cheeks. Shelby crouched by Karen's shoulder and gently lifted the sleepy head, sliding a pillow underneath. The other she placed behind the small of Karen's back. She flicked the blanket out and laid it over her long body, tucking it under Karen's chin. Shelby wasn't sure exactly how old Karen was—around twenty-five she thought—but she looked about eleven as she slept peacefully.

Shelby brushed an errant lock of hair off Karen's forehead and let her finger linger against her temple. Any other time, Karen. Any other time. Drunk or not, Karen was attractive, available, and, she suspected, uncomplicated. But something deep in the back of Shelby's brain was stopping her from taking Karen up on her offer. She couldn't get Eve out of her head.

Shelby leaned forward and lightly brushed lips across Karen's forehead. "Goodnight, kid," she whispered.

IT WAS A beautiful, warm day. Eve sat on her verandah, her laptop open on the table in front of her. She sipped from her glass of iced tea and reread the report in front of her.

A big part of Eve's practice involved consultant work for various lawyers around town, assessing clients who were usually on trial for violent crimes and sexual offences, or both. She adored this part of her work, but it did mean many hours spent writing and rewriting her carefully worded reports on the weekends.

The work had the power to make Eve forget the passage of

time, some days, and this morning was one of those moments. Since breakfast she had worked on one particular report and now it was almost noon. The complete absence of noise from the bottom storey of the house had helped her concentration. At least that was what she told herself. In the end it was her stomach rumbling that made Eve lift her head.

With a sigh she stretched and rubbed the back of her neck. I'm hungry, but can I be bothered getting up and organizing something to eat, she pondered. Eve glanced at the screen of her laptop, re-reading the last few sentences she had written. It was enough to suck her back into the process, her empty stomach forgotten, at least for the moment.

Chapter Three

SHELBY DRIFTED AWAKE as the bed moved behind her. Part of her brain knew that either Rufus had gained a lot of weight overnight, or Karen had climbed in with her. She wasn't awake enough to do anything other than sigh and flutter her eyelashes, however, so when a long, lean arm snaked around her waist and pulled her back against her, Shelby didn't put up much of a fight.

Doesn't mean anything, her mind reassured her. We're snuggling, that's all. No, really, we are. For a few seconds she allowed the pleasant sensations to touch her, the unfamiliar feel of another human against her back a sweet reminder of how long she'd been alone. Nice. Confusing, but nice.

Karen moved slowly against her and before long Shelby felt the unmistakable touch of soft lips on the nape of her neck. Tingles radiated out from the point of contact.

Imagine how much better it would feel if it was Eve's lips.

Shelby's eyes flew open. The thought had come unbidden but clear as a bell and Shelby felt the bottom drop out of her stomach.

"Karrrrrrrennn." She tried to decide whether to push all thoughts of Eve from her mind, or Karen from her bed.

"Mmmmmm?"

"You promised to be good."

Karen's breath was warm on the edge of Shelby's ear. "I promised to be good last night. This is morning." Her hand made a move toward Shelby's breast, but Shelby intercepted her, pulling Karen's hand away and clasping it to her stomach.

"This morning is early afternoon, if I'm not mistaken, and last night was this morning," Shelby said, confusing herself.

"You think too much, Shelby." Karen laid another line of kisses down Shelby's neck, ending just above the collar of her t-shirt.

Shelby groaned inwardly, trying to ignore the strong physical reaction she was experiencing. "Don't you even have a headache?" she said aloud. "You were wasted a few hours ago. I have one and I was drinking Coke all night." She could almost feel Karen grinning.

"Nope, I feel great."

Yes, you do. Ah, youth. I remember when I used to be able

to party all night and still wake up wanting more.

"Karen?"

"Yesssssssss?"

"How old are you?"

"Twenty-three."

Holy mother of God. Shelby winced. Worse than I thought. "You do realize that I'm fifteen years older than you?"

Karen giggled and pulled her until Shelby had to roll on to her back, as Karen leaned over her.

"I don't care how old you are," Karen said, her smile softening as she met Shelby's eyes. "You're hot, Shel, and we could have a lot of fun together. Don't you want to have some fun?"

Yes, yes I do, but... "It's not as simple as that."

Karen leaned closer. "It could be if you just let it be. What are you afraid of? It's not like I'm asking for a commitment."

Shelby recognized how much difference fifteen years could make to a woman's attitude to romance. She wondered how to explain that she wasn't wired for one-night stands, and that commitment would have been easier to accept than a meaningless roll in the sack, no matter how playful it might be. "I know."

"So chill out." Karen pressed closer, kissing the corner of Shelby's mouth with tantalizing care.

Oh boy. The voice in the back of Shelby's head kept telling her she was making a mistake, but it was hard to hear over her body yelling to let things take their natural course. With only a fraction of a second to decide, her body won out, and she found herself responding to Karen's gentle explorations.

It feels so good. So very, very good. Karen's tongue was soft, warm, and far more polite than Shelby had expected. The tentative quality to the kiss told Shelby Karen was less confident than first impressions suggested. Somehow, that made it easier for Shelby to respond and soon she was deeply involved, her arms finding their way around Karen's waist and pulling her closer.

How long is it since I kissed someone, she found herself thinking. Karen's body was a warm weight along Shelby's right side. Too long. Way too long. Karen's leg slipped between her thighs, pressing more insistently. Shelby heard herself groan against the contact.

What if Eve hears us? Shelby's heart jumped as Karen trailed a string of kisses down Shelby's neck to her collarbone. Jesus, shut up, brain, shut up. Desperately she tried to focus on what was happening, tried to get lost in the sensations. Karen was humming softly as she worked her way back to Shelby's mouth and was clearly enjoying herself. *Why can't you be like that, Shelby? Just concentrate for God's sake. It feels good, go with it, damn it.*

Karen's hand found the bottom edge of Shelby's t-shirt and meandered up Shelby's side, until gentle fingertips brushed the outside edge of her breast.

Oh god, Eve, that feels so good.

Shelby's eyes flew open again when she realized what she was thinking and she knew it had to stop. Quickly she squirmed away from Karen's touch.

"Karen, stop. Wait, please."

Karen's head lifted, her eyes glazed with desire. "Wh-what's wrong? Did I hurt you?" She pulled back rapidly.

"No, no, nothing like that. Far from it. I just..."

Karen stared at her, seemingly perplexed by the sudden reversal in proceedings. Shelby felt a stab of guilt even as she scrambled away and out of the bed.

"I...need not to do this right now." Shelby looked down at the frustrated and confused woman sprawled across her bed. "I'm sorry, Kar, honestly. I can't do this right now."

Karen propped her head on her hand and frowned up at her. "Is it me?"

"No. God no." Shelby sat down on the edge of the bed, disconcerted by her rapid change of mind. "You're..." She took in the length of Karen's near-naked body. "You're gorgeous. And that was very...very...enjoyable." She sighed as residual tingles coursed through her.

"Then what?" Karen rolled onto her back and put her hands behind her head, watching Shelby expectantly.

I really need to talk to Eve, Shelby realized. *I can't do anything with anyone else while we have this...this...what...potential? Between us.*

"Karen I don't really know what to tell you," she said aloud. "I'm sorry."

Karen sighed. "No, it's not your fault. I guess I should have taken you seriously when you said you wanted me to be good." She grinned and Shelby felt a wave of relief.

"Mmmm, maybe so. But I wasn't exactly pushing you away for a while there, was I?"

Karen chuckled and then became serious again, looking directly into Shelby's eyes. "So is that it? Or do I have any chance of persuading you back into bed?" She patted the still-warm spot Shelby had recently vacated.

"Not today," Shelby said.

"But not never?"

Shelby smiled. "I just need some time to work some things out, okay?"

Karen tilted her head, clearly thinking about what Shelby was saying. "Okay," she replied slowly. She sat up, wrapping her arms around her knees and smiling back at Shelby. "You'd better call me a cab, then, I guess."

"You're a cab," Shelby said, relieved that she'd at least managed to soothe Karen's ruffled feathers. Now all I need is a cold shower to smooth mine, she thought.

EVE LIFTED HER head when the taxi pulled up in front of the house. Almost immediately she heard Shelby's front door open and seconds later she and Karen walked out from under the shade of the veranda and across the lawn.

Shelby and Karen were more or less the same height and although both had dark hair that hung below their shoulders, Karen's was black, while Shelby's carried auburn highlights that caught the afternoon sun.

As Eve continued to watch, Karen leaned closer to Shelby and slipped her hand through the crook of her arm. Although she couldn't hear the conversation, Eve could see that Karen was speaking intently. Shelby's head was cocked toward her friend, in a listening posture.

Eve didn't quite know what to feel. Whatever happened between them the night before, they were clearly closer for the experience. With a sinking feeling, she watched as Shelby opened the back door of the cab. Karen reached up and cupped Shelby's cheek with one hand, and Eve could see the smile on the young woman's face.

Whatever you're saying, Shelby, you're charming the socks off the women, as usual, Eve thought, with a wry smile. Shelby leaned in and kissed Karen lightly. Oh, I think you may have missed your chance, Eve admonished herself. She dropped her eyes as the kiss lingered, surprised to feel a lump in her throat. Damn.

"SO, DO YOU forgive me for being pushy?" Karen asked as Shelby opened the car door for her. She leaned on the door as Shelby moved closer, the door between them. Shelby answered with a grin.

"Of course," Shelby replied. "It's hard to be mad when someone as gorgeous as you crawls in to my bed. Apart from anything else, it's incredibly flattering."

Karen smiled back and reached up to cup Shelby's cheek with the palm of her hand. "You really are a sweetie, you know?" Her thumb brushed across Shelby's skin gently. "I think I'd like to wait around and see what decision you come up with. Is that okay?"

Shelby smiled softly. "It's not like either of us are going anywhere," she said. It was hard to resist leaning into Karen's touch. "And thank you for backing off when I asked you to. I know I left you hanging."

Karen shrugged and withdrew her hand slowly. "There are worse ways to be left hanging." She laughed. "I'll see you Tuesday afternoon?"

Shelby nodded. "Mmhmm. I'll be there." She ducked her head and kissed Karen, happy to let Karen take the kiss over and dictate the pace. Whatever else she was feeling, Shelby was enjoying the intimacy of physical contact. "Get some sleep," she murmured when Karen finally withdrew.

"You too," Karen replied with a smile. "Bye."

"Bye."

Karen climbed into the back of the taxi and Shelby waved as it pulled away from the curb. As she watched it disappearing down the street, she tucked her hands in the pockets of her loose-fitting pants and contemplated the events of the morning.

"Jesus, Shelby, you've got to get your shit together, here," she muttered. *I mean, what the hell are you thinking?* She turned and walked slowly back toward the house, her eyes downcast. *Karen's smart, attractive, available—and young, god, she's so young—so, why on earth am I fighting it?*

"Good afternoon."

Shelby's head jerked up and she was treated to the sight of Eve leaning against a veranda post, gazing down at her. For some reason the blue of Eve's eyes was particularly vivid and Shelby felt her stomach flip-flop.

That's why, Shelby thought as she gazed back.

"I was just about to make some lunch. Would you like to join me?" Eve asked.

I wonder how long she's been standing there, Shelby thought. *How much did she see? And what is she thinking?* "Thanks. I'd like that."

"Come on then," Eve said, pushing upright. "You can help me throw a salad together."

"Okay." Shelby climbed the stairs to the veranda, her right hand sliding up the wooden banister. She was aware of Eve watching her, a slight smile on her face, and Shelby wondered if her every emotion was readable. God knows, she always did have a fair idea what I was thinking.

Eve walked back inside the house and Shelby followed, wondering where the next conversation was going to take them.

For a few minutes there was no conversation at all, both women preferring the companionable silence as they moved about the kitchen, assembling the ingredients for their lunch. Shelby pulled out plates and cutlery, and began to set the table.

"How's the report-writing going?" she asked, thinking that, at least, would be a fairly safe topic.

"Oh, pretty good," Eve said as she arranged fresh croissants on a large plate. "I've done two. One more to do this afternoon, and I'll be done for the week, with any luck."

"Anything interesting?" Shelby asked. Forks, knives, napkins.

"Mmmm, depends how you define interesting." Eve smiled. "Two pedophiles and a young man who was involved in a murder."

Shelby looked up after she placed a range of condiments in the middle of the dining table. "Involved as in he did it? Or involved as in stood around and watched?" she asked.

"Well, that's the bone of contention, of course," Eve said. She walked around the kitchen island with the salad bowl in one hand and the croissants in the other. "There's some sliced ham and a few different cheeses in the fridge, if you could grab those please." She placed the dishes on the table as Shelby walked past her. "He says he didn't do the actual killing, but was on the outskirts cheering on the ringleader."

"How many were there?" Shelby put the plate of ham down next to the croissants, and then arranged the wedges of brie, camembert and Roquefort around the pastries. "God, I love this stuff," she murmured as she sucked a morsel of the blue cheese from her thumb.

"Four." Eve returned to the kitchen, hooking two wineglasses with one hand as she pulled a bottle of red wine from the cupboard. "He's the youngest of the group."

Shelby sat down and waited for Eve to take her place on the other side of the table. "What's his history?"

Eve picked up a napkin and unfolded it, placing it across her lap. "He's nineteen, been here five years." She handed Shelby the bottle opener, and watched as she started peeling the plastic from the neck of the wine bottle. "He's a Vietnamese refugee," Eve said in answer to Shelby's unasked question. "Speaks hardly any English."

Shelby poured some of the dark, rich red liquid into Eve's

glass and then did the same for her own. "How have you been able to assess him?" she asked.

"I had an interpreter. It certainly made life interesting." She reached for a croissant and broke it apart with her fingers. "Turns out he's been abused pretty much all his life—physically, probably sexually, not that he was admitting that much."

"But you think so?"

"Mmhmm. He's also got a drug habit. Heroin for the past three years or so. And post-traumatic stress disorder. So he should do really well in prison." The last was said with a wry edge that was borne of many years dealing with the justice system.

Shelby thought about that as she cut herself a portion of cheese, and piled some ham onto her plate. "You're trying to get his sentence reduced?"

Eve shrugged. "Yes. He's been given nine years, which is the maximum for what he was charged with. He's appealing the severity." She took a bite-sized portion of croissant and popped it into her mouth.

"Will he win?"

Eve chewed as she thought about her answer. "Honestly? No, I don't think so. The judge in the original case was trying to send a message, and there's no reason to think the appellate judge will see it any differently, no matter what the psychologist says."

"But you're trying anyway." A statement, not a question.

Eve smiled, matching Shelby's grin. "I always try," she said.

The two women concentrated on their food for a few minutes before Eve asked, "Was it a good party?"

Shelby shrugged nonchalantly. "As far as those things go, yeah, it wasn't bad," she said. "Everyone got very drunk, nobody talked about anything sensible at all and Lynne spent most of the night trying to fix me up with Karen."

Eve snorted. "I got the feeling that Karen probably didn't need too much help in that department," she said, softening her words with a smile.

Shelby felt herself her blushing. "That's true." She pushed her food around with a fork for a few seconds. "I'm, uh, sorry if we woke you on the way in this morning."

"You didn't," Eve lied. Another long silence. "So, are you going to tell me any of the juicy details or am I going to have to extract them one by one," she asked.

Shelby looked sheepish at best and uncomfortable at worst. "There's nothing to tell you, truthfully," she said, still not meeting her friend's eyes. "She's too young." A glance up. "She's a baby, Eve—fifteen years younger than me, for crying out loud. She barely knows she's alive."

"Is that a bad thing, grandma?" Eve asked.

Shelby shrugged. "I don't know. She wants to play it light and easy, have some fun, all of that."

"And you don't want to do that?"

"Oh, it's not that so much," Shelby answered. She bit down on the end of a celery stick and chewed thoughtfully. "It's more that I kind of like the way things are for me right now, and I'm not sure 'a bit of fun' is worth disrupting that for."

"Hmmm." Eve buttered another piece of croissant. "The safety of the status quo, huh?"

Shelby grimaced. "Well, when you put it that way, it sounds so...dull," she said. "But yes, I guess so. Sort of."

Chapter Four

Brisbane, Sixteen Years Earlier

INSIDE HER CORNER office, Eve made a few more notes in the file of the client she had just seen, an ex-soldier with post-traumatic stress disorder. He had been one of her first clients when she had launched her practice five years earlier, and although his progress was slow, it was steady. She scribbled quickly, knowing that she only had a short time before her thoughts must turn to the next person. With a satisfied sigh she closed the file and dropped it into her out tray.

Outside, it was a clear, blue day and from her vantage point twenty stories up, Eve had a panoramic view of the city skyline. It was somehow relaxing to be above the teeming streets like this and Eve enjoyed a few moments of head-clearing day dreaming. It wasn't long, however, before her internal alarm clock made her reach for the file at the top of her in tray.

Shelby Macrossan, she read. Not much to review here. The client had been referred by one of the local doctors, but other than the basics of name, address and date of birth — twenty-two, almost twenty-three, Eve quickly calculated — there was no other information. Much the way Eve wanted it. She preferred to make her own assessment of new clients without any preconceptions provided by a doctor, who might or might not know what they were talking about. Eve glanced at her watch. Time to introduce myself.

SHELBY DIDN'T EVEN realize she was chewing her fingernails until she nibbled too far and bit into the quick. She winced at the sting but, truthfully, it was a welcome distraction from the tight knot of tension in her belly. This wasn't Shelby's first attempt at therapy, and the last try had ended badly, so she felt like she was out on a very long limb, over a very long drop.

She shifted in her seat uneasily, and glanced at her watch. Almost 11:35 a.m. So when does this hour start, she wondered. At that moment a door to her left opened and a woman stepped out. Shelby took in a shapely pair of ankles before a voice saying her name pulled her eyes further north.

"Shelby?"

"Um, yeah, hello," Shelby said, unfolding herself from the

chair and standing up in a hurry. She took the offered hand and shook it.

"Hello. I'm Eve." The woman's smile was warm, genuine and stretched all the way to her periwinkle blue eyes. Shelby's butterflies settled somewhat. "Come on in." The psychologist gestured toward her office door. Shelby picked her motorcycle helmet up off the chair next to her and walked through, Eve following behind.

THE OFFICE WAS austere, containing a desk with its accompanying chair, and two armchairs, one of them a recliner. Tucked in one corner was a whiteboard on an easel.

"Take a seat wherever you like," Eve said. "But trust me, that one," she pointed to the armchair closest to her desk, "is the most comfortable."

Eve watched as Shelby dropped her helmet on the recliner and then sat carefully in the other armchair. The young woman was certainly out to make an impression, Eve thought as she followed Shelby into the room. Jeans strategically torn at one knee, a tight-fitting white t-shirt under a leather jacket, and black boots completed a studied image of casual rebelliousness. Shelby's hands rested on her thighs, her fingers drumming a nervous tattoo on the denim.

Eve sat and matched Shelby's open posture. She crossed her legs at the ankles and tucked them under the chair, her hands clasped in her lap.

"What brings you to see me today?" she asked, smiling.

"I guess I haven't been too happy lately," Shelby finally said. "And decided I needed some help."

Decent beginning, Eve decided. Here of her own accord and admitting to needing help. "Tell me a little more about not feeling happy."

Shelby's fingers picked at the frayed edge of the tear in her jeans. "I...um...don't really know where to start." She glanced up and caught Eve's patient gaze. "You're not the first therapist I've been to."

"That's all right," Eve said. She recognized it as the first of what would, no doubt, be a series of small tests. Every new client found ways of assessing if Eve was a good "fit" for them, and it wasn't something that unnerved her, particularly. Being non-judgmental was part of the job. Part of what made the process useful.

"About a month ago I saw someone else," Shelby continued. "She had a crew-cut and a German accent. Told me I had a taboo about touching my mother." She grinned lopsidedly. "She scared the crap out of me, frankly."

Eve laughed. "Well, hopefully I'm not going to do that."

"So far, so good," Shelby replied.

"Why do you think she thought you had a taboo about your mother?"

Shelby tucked a flyaway lock of hair behind her ear. "She told me so, pretty bluntly. I don't know. I guess she was asking me a bunch of stuff about my family. And as there's only my parents and me, it was a fair bet I was going to talk about my mother a decent amount."

"You're an only child?"

"Yeah. I moved out of home about four years ago, and I just moved back in again. It's not working out too well, so far." Shelby tilted her head slightly and looked directly at Eve. "How come you're not taking notes?"

Eve smiled. Nice deflection. "I think it's more useful if we just have a conversation," she said. "I'll make a few notes once we're done and that will remind me of the relevant points next time you come. Assuming that's what you want to do."

"I don't know yet," Shelby said quickly.

"That's okay." Eve turned and poured herself a glass of iced water from the jug on her desk. "Would you like a glass?" she asked.

"Yes, please." Shelby took the offered drink and took a slow mouthful. She watched while Eve did the same, draining hers. Shelby finished and handed the glass back. "You must do a lot of talking all day."

"Yes. But most of my job is listening," Eve said. "What about you? What do you do?"

Shelby's gaze dropped back to her hands. "I'm back at school—that's why I moved home again—studying for my stage management degree. Before that I was a travel consultant." She grinned. "A really bad travel consultant."

"Why bad?" Eve asked.

A shrug. "I'm no salesman. If people don't want to go somewhere, I'm not going to try and persuade them otherwise. It's their money, after all." There was a slightly defiant tilt to the set of Shelby's jaw, almost as if she was daring Eve to challenge her position.

"Sounds like you did the right thing getting out of the business," Eve said, noting her client's almost immediate softening of her body language. *Looks like I passed another test there.* "Was it difficult moving back in with your parents?"

Another shrug. "They were happy about it," Shelby said, not

answering the question. "And I needed the help, financially, so I guess it was for the best." Shelby's downcast eyes and flattened tone told a different story, however. Eve waited, tossing up between asking another question and her instinct that Shelby was close to telling her more. "It's been a bit of a pain in the ass."

"You enjoyed your independence." More a statement than a question.

"Yes. I liked being able to do what I wanted, when I wanted." There was that spark of intelligent rebellion in the brown eyes.

"And you can't now that you're back at home?"

"Not without an argument," Shelby muttered, her eyes again avoiding Eve's. "Or lying." Eve waited, keeping her face and body language attentive. "I...um...I think...I might be, um, gay."

Now we're getting somewhere, Eve thought. "And you think your parents might not be supportive?"

Shelby nodded slowly, and then seemed to change her mind. "I don't really know, anymore. They, um, they caught me. With a woman—well, girl, really. When I was seventeen. I've had a couple of boyfriends since, though. Nothing that lasted more than a few dates."

"And how did your parents react to you being with a woman?"

Shelby sighed and looked out the window, her gaze far away and sad. "It was a bit of a nightmare," she said eventually. "My mother would walk into the room, look at me, burst in to tears and then run away. And then I would catch my dad just staring at me." She looked back at Eve. "That went on for about six weeks until I couldn't stand it any longer and told them that my girlfriend and I had broken up." Her eyes flicked downward again.

"And had you?" Eve asked.

A cheeky grin told her the answer to that even before Shelby replied, and Eve found herself smiling back. "Uh, no," Shelby said. "We pretty much snuck around behind our parents' backs for another six months or so until I turned 18 and moved out."

"And then what happened?"

"Oh, you know how it goes." Shelby sighed. "Bliss for a while. Girl meets girl, girl loves girl, girl meets man of her dreams who just happens to look like the other girl, girl loses girl." Her wry smile spoke volumes.

Eve watched as a range of emotions took their turn crossing Shelby's face. She's smart, this one, she thought. Smart and sensitive and a world expert at keeping her emotions at a distance, using whatever she can. Humor, for instance.

"Tell me more about your parents," she suggested.

Shelby looked at her directly. "Is this the part where you tell me I'm gay because my mother didn't breastfeed me?"

Eve laughed softly. "Nope. I'd just like a clearer picture of them. What do they do?"

"Dad's a mathematics professor at the university, and Mum's a high school English teacher."

"So, a couple of intellectuals."

Shelby nodded slowly. "Dad, sure. Mum not so much, but only because she doesn't think she's smart enough, I think. She sure knows her literature, though. She could talk for hours about Christopher Marlowe." She looked at Eve again. "I hate Marlowe."

"Me too," Eve said. "I was more of a John Donne fan."

"Yes!" Shelby said. "'She's all states, and all princes, I.'"

"'Nothing else is,'" Eve said. Shelby looked at her in surprise. *Gotcha.* "Have you talked to your parents since then about your sexuality?" she asked, refocusing the conversation.

Shelby shook her head. "The only real talk we've ever had about that time was about trust." Eve cocked her head as if she was about to ask for clarification. "At the time," Shelby expanded, "they said the thing that hurt them the most was that I lied to them. And they said it would take a while before they trusted me again. That's one of the reasons I moved out as soon as I could."

"And since you moved back home?"

Shelby sighed. "They want to know where I'm going, when I'm going to be home and who I'm going out with." She looked at Eve and shrugged in resignation. "I can't stand the thought of hurting them again, so I stay away from my usual...um...haunts."

"And what are they?"

"Um...gay clubs...bars...hangouts...you know."

"So if you're staying away from them, you must be staying away from your friends as well."

Another shrug. "Well, a few go to university with me, so I get to catch up during the day," Shelby said. "But, yeah. And...well, I guess I've learned a few golden rules about lying, so I'm better at that than I used to be." Encouraged by Eve's interested look, she went on. "First rule is, when in doubt, tell the truth. Second rule is, if you can't tell the truth, keep the lie simple. Third rule is, if you can't keep it simple, for Christ's sake write it down so you can keep your story straight later." Eve chuckled. "Rules to live by. So what do you think? Am I nuts?"

"No, you're not nuts," Eve said. "But I think you'd benefit from coming and talking with me again. Maybe in a couple of weeks. Would you like to do that?"

Shelby took a couple of seconds to think about it, but then nodded. "Yes, I think so. You seem pretty nice." She grinned at Eve, who smiled back.

"Why, thank you. I try to be," Eve said wryly. Both women stood and shook hands. "It was nice to meet you, Shelby. Talk to my receptionist about booking another appointment."

"Will do. And thanks."

"No problem. Bye."

"Bye."

Eve closed the door behind her new client and sat back down at her desk. She flipped open Shelby's file and reached for a pen. Quickly she jotted down some notes while the session was still fresh in her mind.

Only child, boundary issues, enmeshed with her parents, she wrote. Says she "might be gay", but that's not the real issue. Self-esteem. Parents intellectualize. Emotions kept at arm's length.

THE YOUNG WOMAN sitting across from her looked so miserable Eve could almost feel the ache herself. She and Shelby had developed a good working relationship over the past six months. Shelby had learned to trust her to the point where she was comfortable making herself as open as possible. They talked about anything and everything and gradually, over the months, Shelby's deep-seated loneliness and insecurities had come to the surface under Eve's gentle coaxing. Quite apart from the positive regard she showed around all her clients, Eve liked Shelby. Shelby was intellectually her equal, funny, open and willing to learn, and she showed a social conscience that resonated with many of Eve's own beliefs and values.

Shelby also had a classic case of transference brewing. Those big, brown eyes are telling that tale in spades, Eve thought as Shelby's adoring gaze tracked hers. Right now Shelby was depressed and down on herself in a big way, making her supremely vulnerable and needy. Eve was about her only source of comfort and reassurance and that put Eve at the top of Shelby's hit parade. A dangerous place to be if I'm not careful, Eve contemplated. Especially as I care a lot about her. I need to take care to do the things she needs me to do, not the things I need to do.

They had spent a good part of the last few months trying to find ways of helping Shelby to enforce more boundaries with her over-present parents. That had culminated in a conversation with them in which Shelby had come as close as she ever had to outing herself. But not close enough for her.

"I don't think I did a very good job of it," she said.

"I disagree," Eve replied. "You told them what you needed and you got them to agree to it."

"But I didn't...I didn't tell them the most important thing."

"I don't think being specific about your sexuality was the most important thing," Eve said. "It sounds to me like you made it pretty clear, even if you didn't actually say the words." Shelby continued to watch her hands shredding a tissue, and she sniffled slightly. I need to be sitting closer to her, Eve realized. Is that what she needs? Yes.

Abruptly she stood and pulled her chair closer to Shelby, close enough to touch her. Shelby smiled through the tears that trailed down her cheeks.

"Now I know I'm in trouble," she joked wanly. Eve moved inside Shelby's personal space, took her hand and squeezed gently. Shelby squeezed back. "When you start holding my hand, things must be serious."

Eve smiled. "Sometimes you need it," she said. "And there is such a thing as counter-transference, you know." Shelby tilted her head quizzically, inviting Eve to explain. Part of her is fascinated by this process, Eve thought. And if it helps her to learn to overcome her depression, then I'm all for it. "Sometimes it's hard to tell whether you need me to comfort you, or if it's just me needing to comfort you."

"Does it matter?" Shelby asked.

"Not especially. As long as we keep talking about it and recognize it for what it is."

Shelby rested her head against the back of her chair. "I can't wait to not be your client anymore."

"Well, there's a ringing endorsement," Eve teased.

"You know what I mean," Shelby said. "Do you think we'd be friends if we met outside this place?"

"I'm a terrible friend," Eve said, deflecting the focus of the question. "I'm anti-social. My friends don't hear from me for months and when they do I never want to do anything exciting."

Shelby grinned. "You work too hard."

"So people keep telling me."

"You love it, though."

Eve nodded. "Now. That was a good little distraction. Shall we get back to work?"

Chapter Five

EVE OPENED THE door to her office, shocked to find Shelby hobbling toward her on crutches.

"What happened?" Eve asked. After nearly five years of therapy sessions, this was the first time Eve had ever seen Shelby with a serious injury.

Shelby's face a picture of concentration as she lowered herself into the chair. "Came off the bike," she muttered. "Broke my ankle, took some skin off my leg."

Eve winced as she took her place opposite Shelby. "I'm sorry about that. How long 'til the plaster comes off?" She looked down at the cast, its once-white surface covered in a variety of signatures and drawings. Not to mention ribald limericks, she thought as she read one offering quickly.

"Another three weeks on crutches, then another two or three before the cast comes off," Shelby said. She slumped back in the chair and rubbed her eyes tiredly.

"What did you hit?" Eve asked. "Or did something hit you?"

"Just the road. It was raining and I took a corner a bit too fast, and lost the back end." Shelby glared at Eve, whose tiny smile was the only giveaway in her otherwise patient expression. "Oh, go on, say it. You know you want to. Everybody else in my life is, so you might as well have a go."

"What are they saying?"

"You know damn well what. Sell the bike, Shelby. Sell the damn bike." Eve looked back, placidly. "How many years have I been riding that bike, Eve? Five?"

"Mmmm I think so, yes. You told me that you bought it just before you first came to see me."

"That's right. And how many times have I come off the damn thing in all that time?"

"Twice," Eve replied promptly. "At least, they're the ones you've told me about." For the first time Shelby looked a little sheepish.

"Okay, all right—four times altogether. But the other two I didn't get hurt. Well, not so you'd notice to look at me, at least."

Eve chuckled. "So what conclusion are you drawing from this?"

A long, drawn-out sigh was her answer. "I was thinking of selling it anyway," Shelby admitted. "I'm getting too old to be a biker chick."

"Yes, grandma. What are you now? All of twenty-seven?"

"Oh shut up."

For long seconds they just grinned, enjoying each other's company.

"So, apart from showing off your terribly romantically broken bones, what brings you in to see me?" Eve finally asked. "It's been a while."

"It has." Shelby shrugged. "Just my twice-yearly oil change, I guess." She smiled. "Plus, I have news."

"Tell me, do."

"I...um...I met someone."

"And by the look on your face, I'm guessing it's someone important."

Shelby nodded. "Her name's Amanda. She's a teacher. She's my age. Smart, funny, and she thinks I'm sexy." She grinned again.

"So she has good taste then?" Eve felt a warm sense of happiness for Shelby, who had endured a series of truly ordinary relationships over the years. Early days, though. Play it cool.

"Of course. She's with me, isn't she?"

"So, when did you meet? How?"

"Two months ago, and she came to the show I was managing at the Arts Centre. She knew one of the chorus girls and came back for a drink after the show. But the silly bitch left her standing when someone suggested a party somewhere. And I rode in."

"On your big white charger, no doubt?"

"No, my large red, shiny motorbike, but the effect was much the same," Shelby said, shrugging her shoulders jauntily. "How could she possibly resist?"

"Indeed." Eve laughed quietly, sharing Shelby's bubbly mood. "So where are you at?"

Shelby blew out a long breath. "We're about to move in together."

"Wow." Eve raised an eyebrow.

"I know, I know. But we're lesbians, Doc. Be grateful we didn't do the U-Haul thing in the first week. In a way we're playing against type." She grinned.

"This is a big move for you," Eve said, seriously.

Shelby nodded, following Eve's lead. "I know. But... She hesitated. "This is special. I think...I think she might be the one I'm supposed to be with."

Well, that's a first, Eve thought. Uncharted territory.

EVE RAN A finger down the list of appointments. Nothing really caught her eye until her last client of the day. Shelby.

Something must be up. Eve had seen less of Shelby since she'd been in a long-term relationship with Amanda over the past six years—in fact there had been a couple of years where contact had amounted to a quick hello phone call at Christmas. It wasn't unusual for Shelby to go several weeks or months between sessions, but her last session had been just two weeks earlier. A session so soon after the last one probably meant trouble.

Shelby seemed to have found what she needed from being with Amanda. Something that made therapy unnecessary.

And that's a good thing, Eve thought wryly, recognizing that somewhere inside she'd missed Shelby. That's what it's all about. Help people learn to be happy. Still—she glanced down at the appointment list again—I wonder what's up.

She'd didn't have long to think about it, however, as the first of the day's clients walked into reception. Shelby's problems would have to wait.

Nine hours later Eve scribbled a quick note on the file of her departing, penultimate client. Her stomach rumbled annoyingly mid-sentence. I'd better do something about that or Shelby won't be able to hear herself think over the racket.

She walked out the door of her office to find her receptionist packing up the books in preparation for leaving. Shelby was in a chair in a corner of the waiting-room. Her long legs were tucked up against her chest, her cheek resting on her knee, the picture of misery. Uh-oh. Eve walked quietly over and touched her fingertips to Shelby's sleek, dark head.

"Hi," Shelby said flatly, not moving.

"I just need to grab a glass of water, then I'll come get you, okay?" Eve said quietly, ruffling the soft hair.

"'K."

Quickly, Eve walked into the private kitchen behind reception, closing the door. Her hunger had been overtaken by a gnawing ache that she recognized as empathy for Shelby. But she opened the fridge and pulled out her sandwich anyway, forcing herself to take two minutes to consume a few bites, knowing that her body needed it, even if she didn't think so.

As soon as she was done she moved back into the reception area. Shelby hadn't moved and the misery was washing off her in waves.

"Come on in," Eve said, standing at the doorway of her office. She watched as Shelby unfolded from the chair, almost painfully. Shelby didn't meet her eyes as she walked past and

Eve followed her in, closing the door behind them.

Eve took her seat, watching as Shelby settled into her chair, her eyes still lowered and her posture one of total defeat. For long seconds silence reigned.

"She left me."

The whisper was almost inaudible, but Eve felt the impact. Shelby's face crumpled as the last word passed her lips and Eve was hard-pressed to stop herself from taking Shelby in her arms. Let her dictate the conversation, Eve. Let her. It was hard.

Tears coursed down Shelby's face now, but she still held her emotions in check with almost painful intensity. "Yesterday. I c-came home and half the stuff in the house was g-gone. All her c-clothes. She...she left a note on the c-coffee table." Shelby's breath hitched.

"What did the note say?" Eve felt herself almost holding her breath, anticipating the swelling emotion threatening to break free from Shelby.

Eve watched Shelby's eyes close. "She met someone...else. Didn't say who it is, but I think I know." Eve waited. "We met her a few weeks ago at a party. They were pretty flirty, but I didn't really think about it at the time."

"And this note was the first sign of trouble?"

Shelby nodded. "I thought...I thought things were going really well. It was our sixth anniversary last week."

"Mmhmm, I remember," Eve said softly. "Did the note say anything else?" It was hard to believe Amanda, whom she had met a couple of times and had seemed a reasonable human being, would end things so suddenly.

Shelby's eyes focused on her fingers, which played aimlessly with the drawstring of her sweat pants. "She apologized. Left a phone number so we can talk when I'm ready to." She ran a hand through her hair listlessly. "I don't think she really wants me to call, though."

"Why do you think that?"

For the first time she lifted her brown eyes to meet Eve's gaze. "Because if she wanted to talk about it, she wouldn't have bothered with a fucking note. She would have hung around and had the decency to talk to me about it in person. Don't you think?" There was venom in Shelby's tone and Eve nodded, knowing the anger wasn't directed at her.

"Yes, I do think that."

"I must have done something wrong, Eve." Now Shelby's pleading eyes didn't leave Eve's for a moment, compelling their connection to hold. "Mustn't I? What did I do wrong?"

"Nothing. You didn't do anything wrong."

"Then why? I don't understand why." The dam burst and Shelby began sobbing helplessly, her face buried in her hands. For a few seconds, Eve felt the pain so deeply her own eyes closed, but then she refocused on Shelby. Quietly she picked up the box of tissues on her desk and offered them. Once Shelby took a handful, Eve moved her chair closer and took Shelby's hand.

"I feel sick," Shelby muttered.

"Mmhmm. Do you want a glass of water?"

A shake of the head. "I don't know what to feel, Eve. I can't believe she's gone."

"I don't think you should expect yourself to feel one thing or another, at this point. Just let yourself be whatever you are." There was a pause as Shelby dabbed at her eyes. "What did you do after you read the note?"

"I tried to call her. But she wasn't answering. And then..." She dropped her eyes. "Then I drove around to Michelle's place." A look up. "That's her name...Michelle." She almost spat it out. "But there was nobody there...so I went home again."

"And then?"

"Then I had a glass of Scotch."

Eve nodded. "Understandable."

"Every half-hour.'Til dawn."

"Ah." Eve suppressed a tiny smile. Even miserable Shelby had a sense of comic timing that was virtually unstoppable. It was endearing, but often a hindrance to getting to her real emotions. She looked exhausted. "Did you get any sleep at all?"

"I waited until I could call here to get an appointment, then I crashed."

Eve pulled Shelby's focus back to her. "I'm going to be incredibly boring and suggest that tonight you try and get some sleep rather than drinking."

Shelby nodded. "I've run out of Scotch, so, okay."

"Mmm, I think that's a good thing."

There was a pause and Eve could see Shelby's eyes focus on the far distance. She looked so lost Eve felt a pang of sympathy. "Where did you just go?" she asked softly after a while.

"What am I going to do without her?"

"HELLO." JOE SMILED up at his wife as she walked in the front door that night.

"Hello." Eve tossed her briefcase wearily on the chair and slumped down on the sofa next to him. She dropped her head on his shoulder, eliciting a raised eyebrow from her husband.

"Tough day?" He took her hand between both of his and

rubbed some warmth back into it.

"Good guess," Eve mumbled.

"Want to tell me?" For the most part Eve was adept at dealing with all that her work threw at her, but talking all day was apt to render her monosyllabic in her off hours.

"Shelby," she said. Joe nodded slowly. "Her girlfriend left her yesterday. Rather brutally."

"Not that there's really a nice way of doing it," Joe said quietly, his faint Scottish brogue music to her ears, as usual.

"No. But it was on the brutal end of the spectrum."

"How's she doing?"

Eve sighed and pushed herself upright again, rubbing her eyes wearily. "Oh, she's in about a thousand pieces."

"But fixable?"

Eve smiled back at him, happier than she could say to have his warm familiarity waiting for her at the end of the day. "Always fixable," she said, leaning in to kiss him. "Doesn't mean it's not hurting like hell right now, though."

"Mmhmm, I know." He patted her cheek gently. "You really like this one."

Eve nodded. "I always have. She's got something I really connect with. Potential?" She shrugged. "I'm not really sure I know the exact words for it."

Joe chuckled softly. "You ready for some dinner, wife?"

"Oh yes. And a very large glass of white wine, please."

"Consider it done."

A YEAR LATER, Shelby and Eve faced each other across Eve's office. While Eve was in her usual upright posture, Shelby was sprawled and relaxed, long legs stretched out in front of her, crossed at the ankles. She rested her head on her hand as the conversation lulled for a moment. They were about halfway through a two-hour session, the last of Eve's working day.

"It's good to see you face-to-face," she said, smiling at Shelby.

"Likewise," Shelby said, letting her pleasure at seeing Eve shine in her grin.

For months they had been conducting their sessions by phone, and while they knew each other well enough to make that work most of the time, there were moments when Shelby knew Eve had needed to see her emotions.

"I wish we could do it this way more often," Eve said.

"I could make more of an effort," Shelby said. "But the hours I'm working are too weird. And when you're available,

I'm usually asleep."

Eve nodded. "I know. Anyway, I'm glad you're here today."

It had been a strange year, in many ways, for Shelby. Since the break-up of her long-term relationship she had been by turns vulnerable, lonely, in love with a straight friend, and miserable at the go-nowhere-ness of the relationships she seemed to form with women. The result had been a long series of weekly sessions on the phone, but this was the second time in a row Shelby had managed to make it into Eve's office.

The silence stretched a little longer and Shelby knew from experience that Eve was just waiting for her to push the conversation wherever she wanted it to go.

"I've noticed something lately, and I'm not sure if it's because I've been here so it's more obvious to me, or if it's actually something that's changed," she said, shifting around to face Eve more squarely.

"What have you noticed?" Eve asked.

"You've been much more personal with me. No, that's not quite what I mean. You've related things back to your experience more than usual." Shelby sighed. "No, that's not even it, either, because you've always done that if you've thought it would help me process stuff."

"I think I've related to how you've been feeling more than usual lately," Eve said.

Shelby nodded. "You've said some things to me over the last few sessions that have meant a lot." She paused, suddenly wondering what it was she was trying to say exactly. It wasn't like Eve didn't know what she was thinking. *Maybe it comes down to how I've been feeling lately,* she thought. *Like I'm rapidly running out of people who understand me.*

"Where do you feel like you fit in?" Eve asked, as if reading Shelby's mind.

The answer was surprisingly close to the tip of her tongue. "I don't think I fit in anywhere," Shelby said, her gaze fixed on the toe of her shoe. "I seem to play a role no matter where I am or who I'm with." She flicked a glance and a wry smile at Eve. "Except with you. I'm more myself with you than anywhere else or with anyone else in my life."

"Because I don't judge you?"

"It's not just that, Doc. You show me bits of yourself and even though I know that's part of the way you choose to 'treat' me, I also know that they are true parts of you."

There was a pause as Eve looked down at her hands, clasped in her lap. "Sometimes I tell you things I wouldn't ever tell anyone else."

Shelby was stunned. It was something she had never expected to hear. "Really?"

"Really."

Shelby felt the sting of unexpected tears. "Why do you think that is?" she asked after clearing her throat.

"I don't feel like I fit in very often either," Eve replied quietly, meeting Shelby's gaze. "I don't connect with many people very well. I think that's why you and I have such interesting conversations."

"We have that in common."

"Yes."

"It's lonely."

Eve held Shelby's gaze and nodded slightly. "It can be, yes."

"But you have Joe."

Eve tore her eyes away and gazed out the window at the clear blue skies beyond the walls of her office. "If it helps you any...we've talked many times about Joe, and you know that he's quite ill." Shelby nodded, watching Eve's faraway look. "He's not going to be around forever."

"I know."

"Sometimes I think about how I will live my life after he's gone. And all I know is that it will be very much alone."

It was said so calmly, almost casually, and yet Shelby understood that it was far from a casual statement. "Does that bother you?" she asked around the lump in her throat.

"Most of the time, no."

There was another moment of silence, but Shelby's thoughts were racing.

"This is going to sound arrogant and presumptuous...but..." Shelby hesitated, unsure of just how big a presumption she was about to make.

"Go on."

Shelby sighed. "When it does bother you, I think I'll be one of the people you can call."

Eve's face relaxed into a smile that crinkled the corners of her eyes. "Yes, I think you will be."

Shelby let go the long breath she'd been holding. A tension she hadn't been aware of suddenly released and judging by the relaxation of her posture, Eve had been feeling it too.

"We're just about done here, aren't we?" Shelby asked.

"We still have half an hour left," Eve replied.

"That's not what I meant."

"I know."

Stopping therapy had been on the agenda several times in the twelve years they had been talking, but it had never been a palatable prospect for Shelby. The thought of being without Eve's regular presence in her life wasn't one she had ever relished. But this...this felt very different.

"I don't think we'd be having this conversation if I was going to be your client after this session," she said quietly.

"That's not why I said the things I did," Eve reassured.

"No, I know that. I meant that we're at a point where we can both be ourselves."

"Ah, I see."

Shelby leaned forward, resting her elbows on her knees and gazing pensively at the floor between her feet. "I'm going to miss you for a while," she said eventually.

"And I'll miss you for a while, as well." Eve's voice was soft and gentle, and Shelby closed her eyes, feeling the warmth of the emotion and understanding between them. "But it won't be forever."

"How will I know when enough time has passed?" Shelby asked.

"We'll both know when it happens, would be my guess."

Shelby laughed. "You say that like you've never done this before," she said.

An answering chuckle. "I don't think I have, quite like this, Shelby. As usual, you are proving to be a unique experience."

They both laughed. "Likewise, I'm sure."

With that Shelby knew exactly what to do. She pushed up off her thighs and stood up. She reached a hand down and pulled Eve to her feet. "The sooner we start this, the sooner it will be done and we can have a chat and a glass of wine." She held Eve's gaze for a long second. "Thank you for everything."

Eve kept hold of Shelby's hand, squeezing the long fingers gently. "It's been a pleasure." Then she did something rare, and to Shelby, precious. Eve leaned in and dropped a soft kiss on Shelby's cheek. "Take care of yourself, honey."

"I know how to do that now, thanks to you."

Eve shrugged. "You did the hard stuff. I just nudged you now and then."

A nod of acknowledgement. "Until later, then?"

"Yes."

"Take care, Eve."

"You too."

"Bye."

"Bye."

It wasn't until hours later that Shelby realized she was completely at peace with the decision they had both made. It felt utterly right.

Chapter Six

Present Day

"GODDAMN YOU, YOU useless piece of crap!" Shelby pounded the steering wheel with the heel of her hand in frustration. For the third time in a week the battered moving rust-pile she called a car gave up the ghost, expiring in a shudder of wheezing exhaust when she tried to pull away at the light. And it couldn't have picked a worse place or time to do it.

It was rush hour, that moment on a Friday night when half the population was trying to get out of the city for the weekend, and the other half was trying to get in for a night in the clubs, bars, theatres and restaurants scattered around the metropolis. And Shelby was caught in the middle of it, trying to get out to the Arts Centre, on the other side of the river, in time for the evening's show.

"Damn it." She groaned, leaning on the wheel. Several horns sounded around her as other drivers tried to negotiate the obstacle she now represented. "Yes, thank you," she said dryly as someone's middle finger waved at her from a passing window. "Very helpful." With a sigh she reached down and released the hood, then undid her seatbelt and opened her door, sucking in a breath as a taxi missed her by a matter of inches. "Jesus."

She moved around to the front of the car, ignoring the milling mass of people who swirled around her as the lights at the intersection changed again and allowed the pedestrians to cross. Shelby reached under the front of the hood and found the latch, unclipping and lifting it.

"Right, you bugger, what is it this time?" She stood with her hands on her hips for a few seconds, trying to assess which one of the car's many trouble spots was causing the problem. "Okay, let's try this." She leaned in and began tweaking the battery terminals, knowing that had been the problem the last time.

"Come on, lady, shift it!" came a yell from somewhere behind the car, followed by more leaning on the horn.

"Whaddaya think I'm trying to do, ya buffoon," Shelby said, sticking her head around the side of the hood to glare at her abuser. A few more adjustments and she slipped back behind the wheel. She invoked the names of several saints and turned the key.

Nothing.

"Shit." Shelby glanced at her watch and admitted defeat, knowing that if she had any hope of getting to the theatre in time for curtain, she had to forget about trying to fix the car herself. "Time to leave it in the hands of the experts," she muttered as she reached for her cell phone. A few minutes later, a tow truck on the way, Shelby switched on the car's hazard lights and resigned herself to the passing waves of abuse.

AT THE SAME time, across town, Eve smiled up at the tall man who was walking toward her across the foyer of the office tower.

"Hello, Richard."

Richard Salerio was one of the top attorneys in town, and one of her major sources of forensic work. He also happened to be smart, funny and dashing. Though he was older than her by a decade, his hair was still dark and full with a splash of distinguished grey at the temples. His ready smile greeted her.

"Hello, lovely lady," he said, leaning down to kiss her cheek. "It's good to see you, as always."

Commuters hurried past them on their way home, while shoppers bustled around, making the most of the shops and restaurants that filled the marble-lined space.

"You look wonderful," Richard said, taking Eve's hand and leading her toward the nearest restaurant.

Eve laughed. "You are such an outrageous liar, Richard," she said. "I look like someone who's been working flat-out for the last ten hours."

"You still look wonderful," he persisted. "Come on, I can hear a Chinese meal calling my name, and I know you must be hungry."

"I am," Eve admitted, happily following his lead. Her day had been a strange mix of the routine and the stressful, with one depressed client falling apart completely during a breakthrough session. Eve had a pounding headache, but the prospect of dinner with one of her favorite people was already beginning to dilute its effects.

"Reservation for two in the name of Salerio, thanks," Richard said to the maitre d' who greeted them at the door.

"Ah yes, sir. Follow me if you would." The head waiter picked up two menus and wound his way through the crowded dining room toward a table for two against the front window of the restaurant. "Your usual table, Mr. Salerio, Dr Morgan," he said, pulling back Eve's chair for her.

"Thank you." Eve sat and took the offered menu as Richard settled in opposite her. "How have you been?" she asked. "I haven't seen you since...when was it?"

"That charming serial rapist I was defending three months ago," he said, smiling wryly at her.

"Ah yes. Lovely fellow."

"Not one of my successes." Richard frowned briefly at the memory, before smiling rakishly at her. "Still, it was worth it to spend some more time in your company."

Eve laughed out loud. "An outrageous liar and a hopeless flirt. You're incorrigible."

"How can I not be, around such beauty?"

"Oh, stop it." Eve laughed as the waiter approached. "Shut up and order."

SHELBY JOGGED UP the busy city street, dodging pedestrians as she climbed the hill toward Eve's office block. Her search for a taxi had proved fruitless and she judged it quicker to try one last alternative. It was hard going against the flow of the masses, even thought her wallet was considerably lighter courtesy of the tow-truck driver who had just hauled her car away.

"Jesus, this street doesn't look so damn long when you're driving," she muttered as she ducked around a bike courier who cut across her path. Eve was her last hope for getting to the theatre in time. And that was only a faint one. If she followed her usual pattern, she only took her car into the office about half the time. "Please let today be one of those days."

Finally, she reached the steps leading up to the foyer of Eve's building. As she made her way toward the bank of elevators, past a glass-fronted restaurant on her left, her eye was caught by a familiar blonde head. Shelby stopped and changed direction, though she knew the chances of Eve wanting to interrupt a dinner with — don't know him but he looks like some lawyer, she thought — just to take her to the theatre were unlikely — it was worth asking.

"I'VE BEEN THINKING," Richard said after the waiter had taken their order.

"What about?" Eve took a sip of wine and was surprised when Richard took her hand as she replaced the glass on the table.

"About us," he replied, taking a firmer grip on her hand.

"We've known each other a long time."

"Yes we have," Eve said cautiously, not at all sure she was happy about where this conversation seemed to be going. Still, she left her hand where it was, unwilling to make any quick judgments.

"I was thinking that it might be nice to get to know each other a bit better. Maybe in a more social setting."

"This is a social setting, Richard."

"Yes, but I mean, a social setting where we don't spend all our time talking about the latest nutcase we're trying to save from the maximum security prison."

"Tch, Richard that's no way to speak of the mentally ill," Eve chided him, though she softened it with a smile. It was an old argument between them, though one neither took all that seriously.

"You know what I mean," Richard said. He squeezed Eve's hand. "We like each other, I think." He waited for Eve's nod before he continued. "And I think we could get to like each other a lot more. I'd like to try."

Oh dear. Eve put her other hand over his and patted it gently. "Richard you're a lovely man—" A movement outside the window caught Eve's eye. With a shock, she realized it was Shelby. Damn.

A WAVE OF something that might just have been jealousy washed through Shelby, even as she saw Eve's hand quickly withdraw. Her eyes met Eve's and Shelby forced a wan smile. She waved weakly.

I'm losing my mind, she decided. Of course she's seeing a guy. Of course she is. When has she ever said that women were her thing? Shelby, you idiot. She curtailed her wave, her hand dropping to her side. She could see through the window that Eve was rising to her feet and suddenly she felt the need to get away. Quickly she turned and headed back toward the steps down to the street.

"EXCUSE ME FOR a moment, Richard," Eve said as she stood up. "I'll be right back." She knew the only reason Shelby would be here would be to see her, but the fleeting look of hurt on Shelby's face had said more than words could. Eve felt the bottom drop out of her stomach as she moved to the door of the restaurant. Once outside, though, she realized that Shelby was almost back on the street.

"Shelby?" she called out, but the woman in question was opening the door of a conveniently available taxi even as the word came out of her mouth.

Shelby turned and waved again. Eve watched helplessly as Shelby ducked into the cab and slammed the door shut. What? What was that about? Damn it.

She walked back into the restaurant, nonplussed by Shelby's reaction. Richard smiled at her and raised an eyebrow as she sat down again.

"Was that a client?" he asked.

"No," Eve said. "I'm sorry for just disappearing like that. It was a friend of mine."

"She okay?"

"I'm not sure. But I guess I'll find out later." Eve picked up her spoon and looked down at the bowl of chicken and crabmeat soup that had been delivered in her absence. Silence from Richard made her look up. "She's my housemate. I'll see her at home."

"Ah. I didn't know you had a housemate," he said. "I would have picked you for the type who likes her space and her privacy."

"I do and I do," Eve said. She took a sip of the soup. "Delicious." She was trying to distract herself from worrying about Shelby. "Shelby and I have known each other a long time and our schedules don't actually coincide very often, so it's a good arrangement." *Why do I have the feeling that I just hurt her?*

There was a pause in conversation as they both concentrated on their first courses, Richard tackling a bowl of wonton soup. When they had finished and the waiter cleared their dishes away, Richard again took Eve's hand.

"So, as I was saying." He smiled. "What do you think?"

Eve sighed. *There's just no getting away from this,* she realized. *But I'll be damned if I'm going to hurt him as well, by not being honest...or at least by leading him on.* "Richard..." she began.

"Uh-oh, that's a bad sign," he said wryly.

"You are a dear man and a great friend," Eve said softly, looking him in the eye. "But I just can't. I like where we are right now, and I'm not ready for anything else." *Okay, so not so honest.* "I'm sorry."

He patted her hand gently. "No, don't be sorry," he said, his smile kind, if a little sad. "Thank you for being up-front with me." He withdrew his hand as the waiter returned with their main courses. Richard picked up his chopsticks and waved them at her. "Now, let's enjoy this fabulous food and go on as we always have." He smiled again and this time Eve actually believed it was genuine.

"Thank you, Richard," she murmured.

IT HADN'T BEEN one of Shelby's better performances, she had to admit. She'd arrived about five minutes before curtain, out of breath and frankly, as cranky as hell. Fortunately Karen had taken the reins pre-show and everything was as it should have been. But during the show Shelby was late on one light cue and missed another one altogether.

I'm damn lucky we're well into the run and everyone knows the cues as well as I do, she thought to herself as she sat down in the Green Room after making sure the sets and props were stowed away. She was hot, sweaty and tired. Damn it.

"Hey, boss." Karen slid into the seat across the table from her and folded her hands on its surface. "You look like hell."

"Gee thanks," Shelby muttered. "It's nothing half a bottle of tequila and a shitty night's sleep won't cure." She lightened up enough to throw a weary smile Karen's way. "Thanks for picking up my pieces tonight. I was crap."

Karen shrugged and smiled back. "Eh. We're all entitled to one crap night a run, right?"

"Right. Thanks anyway."

"My pleasure. Instead of the tequila, can I interest you in a cup of coffee and a piece of chocolate mudcake? I think there're still a couple of pieces left."

"That sounds fabulous."

Karen grinned and stood up. "Don't go away. I'll be right back with the goodies."

Shelby watched Karen as she sauntered up to the counter, her tight jeans framing her long legs nicely. It was pleasant viewing, she had to admit. She's not Eve, her mind persisted. But Eve's clearly got other things on her mind and you've been kidding yourself about what could happen there, anyway, let's face it. An image of that day on the sofa when she could have sworn they almost kissed swam in front of her eyes, maddeningly. I know what she said at the time, but...that guy...her thoughts wandered away as the sound of Karen's laugh distracted her.

She smiled as she watched Karen joke around with the guy behind the counter. Eve was virtually pushing me into dating Karen not long ago, she remembered. She might as well have said 'you've got no chance with me, Shelby, just like it's always been.' Karen wandered back, carrying a loaded tray. *So why the hell am I avoiding Karen? Maybe a good time is what I need. And god knows, I do find her incredibly attractive. The age difference doesn't bother her, so why should it bother me?* A decision seemed to click into place for Shelby.

Karen sat down and handed Shelby her coffee and cake. "What's up? You look a lot happier than when I left," she said.

"Oh, I was just thinking." Shelby stirred a spoonful of sugar into her coffee. "Remember that rain check I asked for?"

Karen's forkful of cake stopped short of her mouth and she met Shelby's eyes. "Uh, sure."

Shelby quirked an eyebrow and grinned. "Oh, really?" Karen grinned back. "So...what did you have in mind?"

Shelby shrugged, overcome by a sudden bout of shyness. "This is good for a start," she said, gesturing at the coffee and cakes with her fork.

Karen took a bite and chewed slowly before swallowing. "You said the last time we talked about this..." She smiled. "You said that you had some things to work out. Does this mean you've done all that?"

Shelby pushed a piece of cake around her plate with her fork. *How to answer that...honestly, I guess.* "I...uh...there was someone else." She looked up to meet Karen's eyes. "It wasn't anything serious, hadn't actually gone anywhere. But I needed to figure out how I felt about that."

"And?"

"And, I guess it made me sad." She smiled gamely. "It wasn't a realistic thing, for a lot of reasons."

Karen cocked an eyebrow at her. "And I am?"

"Well, gee, that makes me sound pretty opportunistic, doesn't it?" Shelby said. "I don't mean it that way. I just mean...that...I'm coming out of my funk, I guess."

"Fair enough," Karen said.

"So...we've got a free night on Monday...would you like to have dinner with me?" For the first time in a long time Shelby was looking forward to exploring the possibilities with someone new.

"I would," Karen said. "Then I know a great new club we can try out. I hear the dance mix there is incredible."

"Sounds like a plan."

Chapter Seven

EVE DROPPED HER briefcase and car keys on the chair in the living room, loosening the jacket of her wool suit with her other hand. It had been a pretty routine Monday, but her thoughts had remained steadfastly distracted all day. Since Friday evening's encounter with Shelby, she had barely seen her housemate. Even though it wasn't that unusual for them to not see each other for days at a time, she had the feeling that somehow this was different. She had the distinct feeling Shelby was avoiding her.

Well, like it or not, Shelby, here I come, she thought as she walked to her bedroom to change into something more comfortable. We still need to talk and I know you have the night off, so tonight is it.

A few minutes later she was more casually dressed in jeans and a t-shirt, and standing in front of the interconnecting door that led down to Shelby's flat. One more moment of hesitation and then she knocked twice.

"Come on in," came the muffled response.

"Hi," Eve said as she walked down the stairs into Shelby's living room. She was surprised to see Shelby dressed to the nines and attaching a pair of earrings as she stood in front of a mirror. "You look lovely."

Shelby's reflection smiled at her as she slid her earrings in place. "Thanks. I wasn't sure about these pants." She tugged at the black linen.

"They're good," Eve reassured her. "Are you going out?"

Shelby took a deep breath and turned around to face Eve, who was leaning against the doorjamb, her hands in her jeans' pockets. "Actually, I have a date."

Eve wasn't expecting the unpleasant jolt that gave her, but she managed a smile. "Great. With Karen?"

"Mmhmm. Dinner then dancing." She picked her jacket up from the back of the chair. "Was there something you wanted?"

I thought so, but somehow I don't think I'm going to get a chance to find out. Eve straightened up and smiled. "Not really. I just wondered what Friday was about. You ran off so quickly."

Shelby shrugged into the jacket while studiously avoiding Eve's eyes. "I was running late for the theatre. My car broke down and I was looking for a lift, but when I saw you were having dinner with...a friend..." She glanced up. "I decided not to ruin your evening and just got moving."

"Richard would have understood, I'm sure," Eve said. "But, thank you for thinking of me."

The two women stood in uncomfortable silence for a few seconds, neither really knowing where else to go with the conversation.

"Well, I've...um...I've got to get going," Shelby finally said, picking up her car keys.

"Have a great time. Say hi to Karen for me," Eve said softly, smiling as she watched Shelby head for the door. And goodbye to that.

THE NIGHTCLUB WAS packed to the rafters. Dykes of every size, shape, age and kink swayed, ground and bumped to the outrageously loud house music. Large screens around the dance floor played videos, soft, and, Shelby noticed with a grin, not so soft porn.

"What do you want to drink?" Karen shouted in her left ear.

"Vodka cran," Shelby bellowed back.

"Find a table. I'll get this round."

Shelby nodded and started edging her way through the crowd, searching for any flat surface that didn't already have a woman's backside, drink or purse sitting on it. Finally she found a miraculously unoccupied booth tucked in the back corner of the dance floor. She slid in and settled in to wait for Karen.

It's been a while since I did this, she thought. A couple dancing away to her left caught her eye. Despite the frenetic tempo of the song blasting from the speaker towers, the two women were grinding slowly and intensely to their own beat. Any closer and they'll burst into flames, Shelby thought, grinning.

She spotted Karen making her way carefully through the dancers. She had three drinks in each hand, holding them aloft as she squeezed between bodies. Finally she reached the table and put the drinks down.

Shelby raised an eyebrow at the quantity of alcohol in front of her.

"What?" Karen said, laughing. "The bar was a zoo. I don't want to go back there any time soon."

"Fair enough," Shelby said. She picked up her first drink and took a long swallow. Ah well, she thought. In for a penny, in for a pound.

"Come on," Karen said, grabbing Shelby's hand as a new

song started up. "Time to get your groove on, Shelby."

SHELBY WOKE UP with a jerk. Unfortunately, given the narrow bed she was occupying, that jerk damn nearly sent her off the edge of the bed. It would have if she hadn't been tangled in the long limbs of the woman squeezed in with her. Karen murmured softly in her sleep and tightened her unconscious grip on Shelby.

She blinked in the late morning light, taking in her unfamiliar surroundings. After dancing until about 2 a.m. they had come back to Karen's tiny bed-sit. Shelby looked around, absorbing details she had been too distracted to take much notice of the night before. The flat was filled with all the trappings of youth — television, stereo, computer in the corner, posters on the wall, and second-hand furniture that didn't match. *Ahhh youth, I remember it well,* Shelby thought wryly.

She was hard-pressed to keep the smile off her face, she had to admit. Karen had proven to be a playful bedmate and the night had been exceptionally pleasant.

If not totally satisfactory. Shelby ran her fingers lightly along Karen's forearm. *Can't have everything,* she mused. *Certainly not the first time around.* She chuckled softly. *Or the second and third. She doubted Karen would know, though. Sometimes it was good to have some years under your belt.*

"Good morning."

Shelby twisted slightly to see sleepy brown eyes blinking at her. "Hi, there. How did you sleep?"

"Mmmmm, like a log," Karen murmured, her voice husky. She rolled away from Shelby a little until her back was against the wall. That allowed Shelby to turn in her arms until she was facing Karen. "How about you?"

"Pretty much the same." Shelby smiled. "Thank you for a lovely night."

"Thank you," Karen said, leaning in for a kiss. "Why'd we wait so long?"

Shelby chuckled. "My fault."

"I'm not complaining," Karen said. "You want some breakfast?"

"Love some."

Karen laughed as she realized how tangled up they were. "You'd better move first, or I'll be trapped in this bed for life."

"Your worst nightmare, right?" Shelby extracted herself from the sheets and stood by the side of the bed, reaching a hand down to Karen.

"It'd be pretty good for a couple of days, that's for sure." Karen took her hand and got up. "But I don't like staying in one place for too long."

Shelby watched as Karen scraped together the makings of breakfast, trying not to read too much into her words. She's young, and this is day one. Don't go expecting much beyond day two, Shel, she told herself. Oddly, she found herself quite content with that. Que sera, sera.

EVE PLOUGHED UP and down the swimming pool, following the black lane line, using the monotony of the exercise to blank out her mind. It was the closest she ever came to meditation and was something she desperately needed this morning.

Shelby's car hadn't been in the drive when she had woken, and Eve knew that meant one thing. She was depressingly unprepared for how bad that felt; unprepared to admit how much she'd wanted things to go differently between herself and Shelby.

Up and down, Eve. Up and down.

She didn't know exactly when her feelings for Shelby changed. They had been therapist and client for so long, Eve kept that professional distance strictly intact and it worked very well for them. Yes, there had been counter-transference, but she had expected that, and dealt with many times before.

But now...Now she's reached in and opened up a whole other part of you, Eve admitted. She never really thought of herself as anything other than married to Joe. In truth she never labeled herself in other ways.

Am I in love with Shelby, she asked herself as she continued to plough up and down the pool. It was unanswerable, at least for now. And perhaps there's no need to keep asking it, she realized, sadly. Maybe it's all too late.

Chapter Eight

Two years earlier

SHELBY PICKED UP the phone on her bedside table as she flipped through her address book. It was a long time since she'd called the number she was looking for and damn if she could remember if it was 0144 or 1044.

It was just over two years since she and Eve had terminated their professional relationship. The time had gone quite quickly, Shelby reflected, but in many ways it had been less difficult than she'd expected. She had missed Eve, of course, but that ache was leavened by a strong sense that it wouldn't last forever and there was the possibility of a solid friendship waiting in the wings. In the time since, they'd seen each other maybe three times, all at Shelby's instigation. A lunch here, a cup of coffee there. Pleasant, but the last time was over a year earlier, and there still seemed to be a little distance between them. As if, by mutual, unspoken decision, they knew it still hadn't been enough time gone by.

It's been two years, Shelby thought as she dialed. That should be long enough, surely. And, damn it, I miss her. She waited as the phone rang.

"Morgan and Riley, Margaret speaking." The familiar voice of Eve's long-time receptionist made Shelby smile.

"Hey, Margaret, it's Shelby Macrossan. How are you?"

"Shelby! I'm fine thanks. It's good to hear from you, but I'm afraid Eve isn't here." Her voice suddenly became much more serious. "I'm afraid there's been some bad news."

Shelby felt a cold shot of fear race through her system. "Is she okay? What happened?"

There was a pause and then Margaret cleared her throat. "Joe died. On Saturday."

"Oh my god." Shelby gasped. "I knew he'd been ill but—"

"Apparently things had been going downhill quite quickly the last few months," Margaret said. "Eve left work early on Friday because he had collapsed at the shopping centre and was taken to hospital. Other than that I don't really know the details."

Shelby closed her eyes and tried to breathe normally, but she hurt for her friend. "Damn, Maggie, that's awful."

"He was such a sweet man. We're all really sad about it." There was another pause and Shelby could hear the shuffling of papers. "I've got the details of the funeral here somewhere, hang on. Oh, here they are. Have you got a pen?"

Shelby took a deep breath and tried to get her mind to focus. "Go ahead." Margaret gave her the relevant information and Shelby quickly wrote them down. "Okay thanks. Look, do you think it would be appropriate for me to go to the funeral? I mean, I have no clue."

"Honestly, I don't know what to tell you," she replied. "Eve is such a private person. I'm not even sure if I should go."

Shelby sighed, considering her options. "Thanks, Maggie. I guess I'll send some flowers and a note."

EVE LAY ON the couch, her right arm across her eyes, a damp handkerchief clutched in her fingers. It was the morning after the funeral and she had finally been left to her own devices. She couldn't for the life of her work out whether that was a good thing or a bad thing. On the one hand, she'd had enough of people being kind and solicitous. But on the other, she was now alone in an empty house with nothing but her own emotions to deal with.

She was bone-weary. From Friday afternoon until right this second, five days later, everything had been a blur. Nights spent in the hospital ICU, knowing that she wouldn't get to speak with Joe again, or at least, knowing he would not be able to answer her. And then days dealing with relatives, funeral directors, caterers.

Thankfully the friends and family had stayed around long enough to clean up after the wake, but everything in the house felt wrong. She kept expecting Joe's tall form to come around a corner, or to hear his favorite music coming from his study. But there was nothing but silence and an emptiness she didn't want to touch.

Eve sighed and pulled herself upright. Lying still with her thoughts was driving her insane.

Someone had left a pile of correspondence on the coffee table. A condolence book, cards, letters and notes were scattered across the polished surface. Eve leaned forward and picked one up.

Eve, it read. I'm so sorry for your loss. I wish I'd had the chance to meet Joe. I know he must have been a very special person. If there's anything I can do, please let me know. With love, Shelby.

Eve smiled. Even without the signature she would have

recognized who the note was from.

So typical of you, Shelby, she thought. Sweet and concerned.

She dropped the card back on the pile, losing interest in reading any more condolences. There was nothing she was sure of, no thoughts formed coherently in her mind and she began wandering from room to room. Every space in the house carried memories. Every painting, each vase, each figurine, every piece of furniture held a story, every one of them was a memory of Joe. Part of her wanted to stay and savor every one of them, and part of her wanted to walk away and into the next room, never lingering too long.

Eventually she found herself standing next to the telephone, her hand hovering over the handset. Without giving herself time to change her mind, Eve flipped through the pages of her address book until one page caught her eye. She ran a finger down the page and stopped at Shelby's number.

THE PHONE WAS damn persistent in her dream. Shelby was trying hard to have a conversation with the faceless woman in front of her but the phone distracted her. And distracted her. And distracted her. Damn.

Shelby swam up out of the dream and fumbled for her phone. "Yeah, h'lo?" she mumbled.

"Hello, it's me. I've woken you up, haven't I?"

The voice was very familiar, but it took a good ten seconds for Shelby to realize it was Eve on the other end of the line.

"Yeah...Eve, hi. It's okay." Shelby rubbed her face and tried to collect her thoughts into something usable. "How are you?" Oh, stupid fucking question, Shel. Her husband just died, you idiot.

Eve dealt with the question with her usual grace, however. "All the better for your sweet card," she said quietly. She went on before Shelby could dig herself a deeper hole. "I was wondering if you'd like to come over for lunch. Not that I can guarantee I'll be much company. Are you working tonight?"

Shelby sat up and drew her knees to her chest. "Yeah, I am, but I don't have to be at the theatre until 4 p.m. I'd love to come over."

"Okay then. See you about 1 p.m.?"

"Sure. Would you like me to bring something? You've got enough on your plate without making lunch for me."

Eve laughed softly. "Trust me, there's more leftover food here than could be consumed by a small Third World country. You can help me clear the decks a little."

SHELBY HESITATED OUTSIDE the door to Eve's house. To be honest, she'd been truly surprised by Eve's phone call inviting her to lunch. Just a day after Joe's funeral, Shelby had expected Eve to be surrounded by family and friends, with no thought of ex-clients in her mind.

But here she was. She'd never been to Eve's home before but the casual elegance of the house and garden were as she would have expected. Shelby reached up and knocked on the door.

Almost immediately she heard movement inside and the door opened. Eve looked much as ever — if dressed more casually than Shelby was used to — and only the dark circles under her blue eyes gave any indication that life had been difficult.

"Hello, Shelby," Eve said, with a smile. "Come on in." Once Shelby was inside, Eve pulled her into a close, warm hug. "Thanks for coming. It's really good to see you."

Shelby shook off her hesitation and relaxed into the hug, tightening her arms around Eve and feeling an answering squeeze. "Thanks for asking me. I was thinking about you lots."

They broke apart and Eve looked up at her. "Your card really made smile. And it reminded me that I hadn't seen you in ages."

She led Shelby through into the lounge and Shelby looked around appreciatively.

"This is lovely," she said. "Somehow I always knew you'd have excellent taste." She grinned at Eve who acknowledged the compliment with a nod.

"Well, it wasn't just me. Joe had a lot to do with it."

"I'm sure," Shelby murmured as she sat down on the sofa. Eve lowered herself into one of the matching armchairs close by. "Can I ask you something?"

Eve raised an eyebrow. "Of course."

"Why am I here?" She laughed at the surprised look on Eve's face. "I don't mean in the metaphysical sense, Doc." They smiled at each other. "I just mean...I would've thought that you'd want family and friends around you right now."

Eve sighed. "I've had family around me all week," she said as she relaxed back into the comfortable leather. "It's been a little much, to be honest. If I had a dollar for every time someone asked me how I'm doing, I could put in that games room we were always..." She swallowed, her gaze flicking away from Shelby. She shook her head and cleared her throat. "And Shelby...I do consider you a friend. I know that's a strange thing to say, given that we've hardly begun to get to know each other outside therapy."

"It does feel a little odd," Shelby admitted. "We've known

each other a very long time. But we've hardly ever..." She left the sentence unfinished, uncertain of what she really meant.

"My fault. There had to be enough time gone past before we tried to start a new direction."

Shelby nodded. "And I understood that. I guess it just surprised me that you would choose now to start."

"Why? Because I should be up to my ears in grief?"

"I guess so, yes."

Eve's smile was sad. "And I am. But I think what I need right now is conversation and none of the expectations that come with the family members and people who consider themselves to be my friends. Does that make sense?"

Shelby thought it did, and she had a theory about why. "I think so. Is it maybe that you need to feel in control. And maybe that's a bit easier with an ex-client."

The truth of that pulled a self-deprecating laugh from Eve. "Sometimes you are scary smart, do you know that?" Shelby chuckled. "When you put it like that it doesn't exactly make me feel proud of myself," Eve admitted. "Not a great way to start getting to know each other."

Shelby brushed it off with a wave of her hand. "Don't worry about it," she said. "I don't have a problem with it, and we have to start somewhere. Just don't ask how everything makes me feel."

They both laughed. "Thank you," she said aloud. "Now come on into the kitchen and let's see what we can rustle up for lunch."

IT WAS A most excellent meal, Shelby decided. They feasted on leftover food from Joe's wake and downed a bottle of quality white wine. The conversation flowed easily between them—as it had always done, but now Shelby found that her former therapist was much more relaxed with her, and more inclined to voice her own opinion instead of reflecting Shelby's. *I like that, and I like her.*

They lapsed into comfortable silence, both sipping their wine and listening to the classical CD Eve put on when they moved back into the lounge.

After a few minutes, Eve turned to her younger companion. "Shelby, can I tell you about Joe?"

Shelby smiled. "I'd love you to. I wish I'd had a chance to meet him and get to know him. I mean, you've always told me little things about him—when he was sick, and stuff—but I feel like I missed out on really knowing a top bloke. So, yes, please do."

Eve shifted in her seat, making herself more comfortable. "It's been quite strange," she said quietly. "Ever since last Friday, I've been surrounded by people who knew him very well, so there wasn't much to say. I wanted to talk about him, but everyone has been on egg shells with me, and it's been...awful."

"How did you meet?" Shelby asked. She was hungry to know more about this woman she'd bared her soul to for more years than she could remember.

"He was the principal of the first school I taught at," Eve said, smiling at the memory.

"I'd forgotten you were a teacher. Was it love at first sight?"

"God, no." Eve laughed. "He was just my boss for ages. I was too busy trying to figure out what on earth I was doing standing in front of a classroom full of sweaty, cranky eight-year-olds to really notice him much. I read his memos, though."

Shelby leaned back in the sofa and stretched her legs out. "Somehow, I bet he noticed you." She was trying to imagine a younger version of the woman sitting next to her. *I would certainly have noticed you.* "And what were you doing standing in front of a roomful of sweaty kids?"

A wry smile was her answer. "Rapidly deciding that I'd made a grave error of judgment," Eve replied. "Try to imagine. Late November in outback New South Wales, in an unairconditioned classroom with thirty-six of them." Eve shook her head at the memories. "It was a nightmare."

"I'd rather not imagine if you don't mind." Shelby grinned at her. "Tell me more about Joe."

Eve kicked off her sandals and rested her head on her hand, her elbow on the arm of the sofa. "One day he asked me to hang back after a staff meeting," she said. "Next thing I knew we were having dinner together." She smiled at Shelby. "It was comfortable and easy."

"No grand passion?" *A cheeky question, Shel.*

Eve laughed quietly. "Oh there was plenty of that," she said. "But that wasn't what made it special."

"No?"

She shook her head. "No." She paused. "A lovely bonus, certainly." Another smile. "I was safe with him."

Shelby nodded, completely understanding. It was something she had always searched for in a relationship, above all else. She wasn't surprised to find the same need in Eve. "What did he like?"

"Many, many things. He played a lot of sport when he was younger. Watched a lot of it when he couldn't play anymore."

Shelby grinned, knowing Eve's aversion for all things competitive. "How did that sit with you?"

"I learned to score at cricket so I would see more of him on the weekends." She smiled. "Bet you didn't expect to hear that."

"You're right. I can't even begin to imagine it." Shelby laughed.

"Well, I did. But there were plenty of other things we both loved. Music, theatre, books. Our politics were pretty compatible and the age difference didn't seem to matter much."

"How much older than you was he?"

"Twelve years. It certainly didn't bother me, but my parents were worried...right up until the moment they met him. Then he just charmed my mother and kept my father talking about sport, so there was no time for either of them to do anything else but like him."

"Smart guy."

"Oh yes," Eve said. "Very. But he was just being who he was."

Shelby found she had a thousand questions about Joe. For years he'd been a part of the conversations she and Eve had shared but most of the time, digging too deep produced a deflection from Eve. Now all the things that Shelby had been curious about over the years came back to the surface and she didn't feel like she had to bite back the questions anymore.

They talked for hours, Eve sharing her memories of Joe, Shelby listening and prompting for more as the minutes ticked past. It was getting late in the day, and Shelby was uncomfortably aware that she would soon need to leave for the theatre. It was the last thing in the world she wanted to do.

"Gosh, Shelby, you'd better get moving," Eve said after a glance at her watch. "You don't want to be late. Not that I want you to go, to be honest."

"Y'know, I don't have to go," Shelby said, sensing the vulnerability of her friend. "It's not like I'm running the show or anything. They can get another crew member in easily."

"Oh, I can't ask you to do that," Eve said. "I have to be alone some time. And you need to go to work. Don't worry about me."

Shelby looked at Eve and decided she wasn't fooled for a second. "Well, I don't want to go either." She folded her arms and crossed her legs. "In fact, I just decided I'm not going to go to work tonight. They can find someone else to do my stuff. Where's your phone?" And with that she bounded out of the sofa and made for the telephone. "Let me give the stage manager a call and then I'm going to make us a cup of tea."

"Shelby..."

"Don't argue," Shelby said as she punched in the number.

"Thank you," Eve said quietly. "Safe," she murmured.

"Done," Shelby said as she replaced the handset. "I am officially suffering from a killer migraine." She grinned. The answering smile from Eve warmed Shelby's guts. "I'm all yours. Tea?"

"Yes please."

LATER, THEY SAT next to each other on the sofa, feet up on the coffee table, shoulders brushing.

"Honestly, I was surprised that your family wasn't hanging around a little longer," Shelby said as she sipped her cup of tea.

"I managed to persuade them not to. But—now that I have a night to face—I...don't know if..."

"I'll stay as long as you want me to, y'know."

"Joe used to say that I'd be relieved once he was gone because then I could finally get the peace and quiet I crave when I'm not working." Shelby watched the faraway look in Eve's eyes. There was a shimmer of tears there. "But there's a difference between silence when someone you love is nearby and silence when he's...not..."

"I would imagine so."

"You spend a lot of time alone."

Shelby laughed wryly. "I'm used to it, and sometimes even that isn't enough to make it...enjoyable."

A tear drifted down Eve's cheek. "Sorry." She brushed it away hastily.

Shelby took her hand and squeezed it, half-expecting Eve to pull away, but instead she felt the grip on her fingers tighten. "You don't have anything to apologize for," she said.

"It's not what you expected though."

"I didn't have any expectations for today, Eve, honestly. Other than wanting to pay my respects." Eve looked at her, more tears threatening to spill over.

"I'm not feeling very counselor-like right now." Eve gave Shelby a wan smile.

"Good thing. You're not my counselor anymore."

"No, I'm really not, am I?"

"Nope."

Eve sighed and rested her head on Shelby's shoulder. It was so unexpected that Shelby found herself holding her breath. She released it slowly and tried to relax. It wasn't that she was uncomfortable with the way the conversation had gone—exactly the opposite. But if Shelby was truly honest she would admit that she had expected nothing more than a quick visit with someone she would have to spend time getting to know again.

This is...really, really...nice, she thought. I'm glad I'm here. I'm glad I sent that note. And I'm very glad I quit therapy when I did. She relaxed and rested her cheek against the top of Eve's head. And I'm so glad it's me she wants to spend this time with.

Chapter Nine

EVE BLINKED. SHE was disconcerted to find herself lying along the sofa, her head resting on Shelby's thigh. How long have I been asleep, she wondered. A gentle snore from behind her head told her she wasn't the only one who had fallen asleep.

Slowly she rolled up into a sitting position and smiled as she looked at her friend. Shelby was deeply, although uncomfortably by all appearances, asleep, her head resting awkwardly on the back of the sofa, her mouth slightly open.

"You're going to regret that in the morning, Shelby," Eve murmured. A glance at Shelby's watch told her it was just after 1 a.m. "Well, I'm not sending you home at this hour, even if I wanted to." Eve stood and looked down at her. She felt a wave of affection. "Shelby, Shelby, honey."

Shelby snored on, her exhalations puffing out her cheeks softly. Eve reached down and took her hand, shaking it gently. "Shelby."

"Wha-buh, uh, hi." Shelby rubbed her face. She looked around and tried to clear her mind. "What happened?"

"We fell asleep," Eve said. "Me first, I think." She was rather surprised that her mind had allowed her to do that. She'd been expecting sleep to be more of a stranger, at least for while.

"Yeah, you did," Shelby said. "I wasn't far behind you, though." She smiled up at Eve. "You okay?"

"Just really tired. Come on, let's sort you out a place to sleep."

"I'm okay here."

"Don't be silly. There are two spare bedrooms. There's no need to be uncomfortable. Come on."

Shelby didn't argue any further. She flexed her neck as she stood and followed Eve down the corridor.

"Here you are," Eve said, leading the way into a neat, small bedroom in the back corner of the house. Shelby sat down on the bed while Eve went to a cupboard and pulled out fresh linen. "My sister used this room until this morning, so let's just give it a quick change."

Shelby yawned and stood up again, following Eve's lead as she began to strip the bed. Three minutes later they had it remade and they stood facing each other.

"You going to sleep all right?" Shelby asked softly.

Eve smiled. "Actually, I think so, yes. I'm at the point where my brain's about stopped."

"Probably a good thing, for right now," Shelby replied. "Come and get me if you need anything."

Eve stepped forward and pulled Shelby into another hug. "Thank you for being here," she whispered.

"Thank you for letting me be," she answered. "I'm glad my being here helps."

Eve stepped back and nodded. "It does." She smiled again. "Good night."

"'Night."

EVE STOOD IN the doorway of the master bedroom and looked around. For the last few months she had slept in one of the spare rooms. Joe had been a light sleeper and in some pain, and they agreed that for the sake of Eve's sleep, and his need to get up and move around through the night, sleeping apart made more sense.

Now she was at a loss to know what she wanted to do. On the one hand, most of her things were in the other room. She was used to sleeping there. On the other, this room was filled with Joe's presence. His clothes, toiletries, a pile of books on the bedside table. Eve gasped slightly at the sight of his beaten up old slippers, peeking out from under the bed.

Suddenly, all she wanted was to crawl into the bed they had shared for the best part of 30 years. Kicking off her shoes she crawled up the bed and slid between the sheets.

"Oh god." She hadn't expected the scent of Joe's aftershave, still present on the pillows and sheets. It undid her, completely. Eve pulled his pillow into her as she curled up on her side, hugging it close and burying her face in its softness. She breathed in his scent and, finally, let the tears fall freely. It was a release she had needed for days, had found impossible with a house full of people. But now it came, raw emotion that burned her throat and swamped her senses. And she let it. Until finally she drifted into a deep sleep, wrapped in her memories.

SHELBY WAS WIDE awake. She could hear Eve crying across the hall, a low keening that tore at her heart. She sat up in bed and pulled her knees to her chest, hugging them.

Do I go to her? The sound was giving Shelby goose-bumps. I've got to go to her, surely? But something held her back. She rocked back and forth, listening. Jesus. Think Shelby. What would she want?

Shelby looked around the room. Her sister was here. And I'll lay dollars to doughnuts Eve didn't cry like this with her family around. She had no idea how she knew that but she was sure, somehow, that she was right.

Leave her be, Shelby, she decided. It's enough that you're here. She's crying even knowing you're here. This is the way she wants it to be. Let her be.

It wasn't easy. Shelby could swear she felt every sob in her bones. But gradually it seemed Eve exhausted herself. Shelby stretched out, trying to relax muscles that had cramped up while she listened. Finally, she too, let sleep take her over.

THE SMELL OF frying bacon dragged Shelby from the bed. She pulled on her jeans and padded out into the living area where she found Eve sliding fried goodies on to a couple of plates.

"Well, good morning, sleepyhead," Eve said, smiling at her guest, who looked disheveled.

"H'lo there. Damn, that smells good." Shelby managed a sleepy grin. Eve was wearing a long, silk dressing gown and Shelby's brain was trying hard to correlate the fourteen years of her experience with the psychologist with the woman standing in front of her, flipping fried eggs. Damn, who knew she'd look this good first thing in the morning, her rebellious mind insisted on thinking. Oh, hush. Quit being inappropriate, for god's sake. "Can I have two eggs, please?"

"Tch, woman, have you no respect for your cholesterol?" Eve said it with a smile, though, and promptly put another egg on Shelby's plate.

"Not yet, nope." Shelby took the plate from Eve and placed it down. She took in a long, appreciative sniff. "Yum. How did you sleep?"

She watched Eve hesitate momentarily. And then decide it was okay.

"Actually, pretty well," Eve said, catching Shelby's eye. "Eventually."

Shelby nodded. "Good. Me too."

Eve sat down opposite her across the breakfast bar. "Good. So, what's on your agenda today?"

Shelby grimaced. "Ugh. I have to start looking for somewhere to live."

"Really? How come? I thought you were still living down the coast."

"Yep," Shelby said around a mouthful of bacon and egg. She chewed and swallowed. "But the owner's decided he wants to live there himself. And he's given me a couple of weeks' notice."

"Wow. That seems a little unfair."

Shelby shrugged. "He's kept the rent low for the last four years, so I guess he's entitled to do what he wants," she said. "Not much I can do about it, anyway. So me and the boycat are going to be homeless unless I find something pretty soon."

Eve smiled. "How is the boy?"

"Feisty as ever. Take a look at this." Shelby held out her right arm and turned it palm up. There was a long scratch down almost the entire length of her forearm. Eve winced.

"What did you do to deserve that?"

"Got between him and his kibble."

"Ouch."

"Oh yeah."

"Is it going to be hard to find a place that will let you have a cat?"

Shelby nodded. "Yeah. Although he's an indoor cat, so maybe I can sneak him in and not tell anyone. But it's pretty hard to hide the bags of kitty litter I bring in every week." She laughed.

Eve put down her cutlery and walked into the living room. "Come with me, Miss Macrossan," she said, gesturing to Shelby to follow her.

Curious, Shelby did as she was told and followed Eve across the large living room to a door. Eve opened it and led the way down a short flight of stairs. As Shelby reached the bottom of the stairs she realized they were in a small apartment, complete with its own kitchen.

"There's the bedroom through there," Eve pointed to the right. "And there's an en suite off that. And it has its own front door and key, for complete privacy." She stood, arms folded as Shelby wandered around, taking it all in. "What do you think?"

Shelby did a double-take. "What do I think? You mean...me? Move in here?" Eve nodded. "Wow, Eve..." Shelby turned a full circle. The apartment was small, but by no means cramped. Well-designed, airy—you'd never know there was a whole house on top of it. She turned around to Eve and grinned. "I'd love to. Yes." It was her turn to hesitate. This was a big step for them both. "Are you sure?"

"Yes. Wouldn't have suggested it if I weren't. How much rent are you paying now?" Shelby named the amount. "Okay, but that's for a three-bedroom place, yes?" Shelby nodded. "So let's halve that."

Shelby was stunned. "That's not enough, Eve," she protested, but Eve already had her hand up to stop her.

"Don't argue."

"Done."

Chapter Ten

Present Day

"HI, THIS IS Karen. I can't take your call right now. Please leave a message and I'll get back to you." Shelby waited for the tone.

"Hey, it's me," she said. "Give me a call. I've got some news about the tour. I'm at home all night, or you've got my cell number. Bye."

She hung up and tapped the phone's handset absentmindedly. It had been three weeks since the night she and Karen had spent together, two weeks since the show had closed its run at the Arts Centre. Since closing night she hadn't heard a word from Karen, but she had resisted the urge to hunt after her.

Maybe I'm missing something here, she thought. But wasn't she the one who crawled into my bed?

She tucked a lock of hair behind her ear and wandered back to her chair in front of the TV. Ah well, at least I had a good excuse for calling her. Shelby reached for the hard copy of the email she had received from her boss, the theatre company's general manager, that afternoon.

"Shel, we're taking the show on the road," she read again. "Six weeks from a week on Monday—starting in Cairns and heading west to Mt Isa, back through the mining towns to the coast and then down through Mackay, Rockhampton, Bundaberg and Maryborough. Get your crew together and let me know who can and who can't—it's short notice, so no harm, no foul, if anyone can't make it—there'll be no penalty. But you need to let me know so we can plug the holes. And here's the really good news—we're going by train! I know, you don't have to tell me how much that sucks, but it's the only way we can make it a viable proposition, and the powers that be mean for us to make some money on this trip. Talk to you Monday. Gil."

"Ugh." Shelby tossed the piece of paper into the air and watched it float down on to the carpet. Train was not her preferred form of travel, particularly when that travel involved moving a complicated set, props, costumes, lighting, orchestral and sound equipment, and a bunch of silly actors. Usually the theatre company would hire a semi-trailer or two and a coach for the humans, but this particular production was proving to be a law unto itself. "Bloody bean counters," she muttered.

In chartered vehicles she had total control of the what, when, how and who, but using the state-run railway meant a whole new level of bureaucracy to wade through every time she had to load and unload her people and stuff.

Shelby had already talked to the props master, costume designer and lighting guy, and they were essentially ready to go as soon as their gear could be loaded. Most of the crew was also available, but Karen and two others had not yet gotten back to her.

Most of her crew were not on salary to the theatre company, but were contracted on a show by show basis, and it wasn't unusual for them to have moved on to another show with another company once this production had finished. So far, she had lucked out, and had signed on most of her original group.

She had no idea if Karen had lined up some other work. On the one hand, Shelby hoped she was available, because she was good at what she did. On the other...

"...on the other hand, I have no idea what I think about any of that," she murmured, as she reached for the TV remote. A knock on the interconnecting door to the main house stopped her. "Come on in," she called out.

Shelby looked over her shoulder to see Eve open the door and wander down the stairs. In her arms was a very smug black cat.

"Hello," Eve said, with a smile. "I was wondering if you were missing a certain four-footed friend." She walked over to the large beanbag on the other side of Shelby's chair and lowered herself into it. Rufus took the opportunity to snuggle into the beanbag, lying back against Eve's side and looking over at Shelby with a languid, sleepy look. Both women chuckled.

"I was starting to wonder where he'd gotten to," Shelby said. "What trouble has he been up to? Did he destroy anything valuable?"

Eve settled back into the beanbag and scratched the cat between his ears. "Just a scrunched-up draft copy of a report I was writing," she said. "Apparently it was posing a threat to the known world and Rufus here saw himself as our only chance."

"Ah, the Mighty Hunter in action, eh?" Shelby chuckled at the relaxed attitudes of both the cat and the woman stretched out in the beanbag. "You look very contented," she observed.

"I've had a good week," Eve replied. "Remember that Vietnamese guy?" Shelby nodded. "His sentence was reduced on the strength of my report."

"Hey, that's great," Shelby said. "Well done, you."

"Thank you. I'm kind of pleased with myself, to be honest."

"Sounds like you have every reason to be." Rufus rolled over and allowed Eve to turn her attention to his belly. "Tch, he's got you wrapped around his little paw, y'know."

Eve looked up at her and laughed. "Like he doesn't have exactly the same effect on you." For another minute or so silence reigned as both women watched the cat enjoying every bit of the attention he was getting. His purr was the loudest thing in the room. "What about you? How was your week?" Eve asked.

"It was going great until about four hours ago when I got the word that we're taking the show on the road in a week," Shelby said, grimacing at the thought of the amount of work she had to get through in the next seven days. "The details are on that piece of paper." She nodded in the direction of the email on the floor. Eve reached down, picked it up and started reading.

"Wow," she murmured. "Six weeks."

Shelby put her hands behind her head and stretched her legs out with a sigh. "Yeh, I know. Is it okay if I leave that little bugger," she nodded in the direction of the cat, "in your hands, for all that time? I know it's a pain, but I can get someone in to cat-sit, if you'd rather."

Eve shook her head. "No need. I'm happy to. He seems to like me." She tweaked the cat's ear.

Shelby snorted. "He ought to. You've been giving him seconds every day for two years. Of course he likes you." She grinned. "Don't tell me you're not the biggest softie on the planet."

"Guilty."

Shelby knew Eve and Joe had dogs and cats all their married life until his illness made it too complicated. It had been fun watching Eve fall in love with Rufus.

"So, I was kind of surprised to find you at home on a Friday night," Eve said, changing the subject.

"Yes, well," Shelby said. "The season is over, and my legion of friends and lovers would appear to have deserted me." The words had an edge, even though she said them jokingly. "I figure it's my usual animal magnetism at work."

She caught Eve smiling at her. This was the point where they always walked a fine line. Shelby knew Eve was trying to be a friend, without sounding like a therapist, and she was trying not to react like a client. Over the last couple of years they'd had plenty of opportunities to learn how to do it, but sometimes it was easy to fall into old patterns.

"You never did tell me how things went with Karen," Eve said.

Shelby laughed. "Not a lot to tell, apparently," she said

wryly. "Would you like a cup of coffee?" At Eve's murmured assent she stood and walked into her kitchen. "Basically we had one night together, then the show ended and..." She shrugged, and then reached for the coffee mugs on the shelf above the sink.

"No contact at all?"

"Nope." Shelby unscrewed the lid of the coffee jar and spooned a helping into each mug. "But now she has to call me back about this tour thing." She glanced up at Eve. "The joys of getting involved with someone you work with."

Eve pushed herself up from the beanbag and came over to the counter as Shelby filled the kettle and switched it on. "Seems a bit rude," she said.

"Mmhmm. But I'm not going to chase it," Shelby said. "It was only ever supposed to be a bit of fun." Their eyes met and again. "Her definition, not necessarily mine."

"I was going to say. That's never been your style."

The kettle whistled and Shelby poured the boiling water into the mugs while Eve took the milk from the fridge.

"Not usually, no, but for some reason I thought I was up for it. I must be losing my touch, though. One night in bed with me doesn't usually chase the women off quite so quickly."

"Tch." Eve batted Shelby's shoulder with a convenient tea-towel. "Stop it, you."

"I was kidding, I was kidding." Shelby laughed, handing Eve's coffee to her.

"Mmm, not so much, I'm thinking. Don't forget who you're talking to."

"Yes, doctor." They were saved from further discussion by the ringing of the phone. "Oh here we go," Shelby muttered as she walked to the phone. Sure enough the call identification told her it was Karen on the line. "Figures she calls me straight back when it's about work."

"I'll leave you to it," Eve said, taking her coffee and walking back up the stairs to the main house. "Come tell me what happens."

"Okay. See ya." Shelby picked up the phone. "Hello, Karen."

EVE HEARD SHELBY'S front door slam and looked up in time to see her climbing into her car and backing down the driveway.

"I guess Friday night is looking up," she murmured as Shelby drove away. Chances were good, she knew, that it was Karen Shelby was going to meet and she felt a pang of worry for her. *I want it to be a good thing between them, honestly, I do,* she told herself. I don't want her to be hurt. Again. But she also had to admit there was a spark of self-interest in wanting Shelby uninvolved.

Sometimes Eve wondered why she didn't push the issue with Shelby. After all, it's not like there wouldn't be some interest there, she thought as she folded her laundry. But every instinct she had also told her that letting things run their natural course was the best thing to do. When it's right, it's right.

A knock at her own front door brought her out of her reverie. As she walked down the hallway toward the door a very familiar silhouette was backlit by her porch light. "Oh Richard, not now," she muttered. With a sigh, she pulled open the door.

"Good evening," Richard said. In his hand was a bunch of flowers. "I know what you're thinking," he said quickly, before Eve could make any response. "You're thinking, what's this rude, persistent oaf doing on my doorstep unannounced."

Eve chuckled, finding her old friend's charm and winning smile easy to accept. "You're not an oaf, Richard. Come on in."

"WHY ARE YOU hassling me about this?" Karen said. She wrenched the screw-cap off a stubby of beer and threw it into the kitchen sink.

Shelby was completely perplexed. "In what way am I hassling you, Karen?" she asked. "You invited me over, here I am. I've already explained that there's no problem if you can't come on the tour. So what's the drama?"

"I'm not talking about the damn tour," Karen snapped. "You've been hassling me about us."

Shelby raised one eyebrow. "Hassling you? I've called you twice. And one of them was tonight, about the tour. How is that hassling?"

"It just is." Karen walked back over to the sofa and slumped down into it. She began tearing away at the bottle's label with restless fingers. Shelby could almost discern a pout, she was sure.

Shelby reached out with an outstretched foot and nudged Karen's knee with it. "What's really going on, Kaz?" she asked gently. I can think of few theories, but I'd rather coax it out of her, she thought.

"I just wanted to have fun while the show was on," Karen replied. "I thought you knew that."

Shelby nodded. "I did know that," she said. "But I didn't expect that the end of the show would mean the end of our friendship as well as the end of us sleeping together." There was a pause as she watched Karen continue to shred the label. "I guess I don't really understand how you thought that would be, given we also work together. And work together pretty well, what's more."

Karen glared at her. "Well, I guess you didn't really think it through either, then, did you?"

Fair call. "Probably not, and given I'm technically your boss, I guess that was pretty irresponsible of me." Shelby knew that was only half the truth, but the last thing she'd expected was this kind of argument. "Are we really going to turn this into a sexual harassment thing, Karen? 'Cos honestly, I'm not sure that's a particularly fair thing, and I thought we knew each other better than that."

Karen sighed. "Yeah, I know. No, of course we're not." She turned to face Shelby and tucked one leg up under herself. "I'm sorry. I know I'm the one who started this. And I really like you, Shel, really I do. And I really like working for you."

Shelby smiled, even though she knew what was coming. "Well, both those things are good to know," she said.

"I can't come on this tour because I was offered the top job over at the Repertory Theatre for their next production."

"But that's great, Kaz—well done, you." Shelby grinned. "You didn't need to worry about telling me that, though. You deserve it."

"Thanks." Karen reached over and took Shelby's hand, squeezing it gently. "I want to work with you again, though, if we can get the timing right."

"No problem at all. There's always a spot for you on my crew, you know that."

They fell into silence, their gazes holding for several seconds.

"How do you feel about break-up sex?" Karen finally said, with a grin.

Shelby laughed. "You're incorrigible." She waited a beat. "Okay."

"HI, DAD." SHELBY lifted the latch on the gate and stepped through into her parents' garden.

"Hello, sunshine." Ned Macrossan, a stocky man about Shelby's height, pulled her into a gruff embrace. "Give me a hug before the dog comes and leaps all over you."

Shelby chuckled, knowing how true that was. Her retired parents were proud owners of a rambunctious two-year-old Labrador pup who was already corkscrewing his way across the lawn toward them.

"How've you been?" her father asked, holding her at arm's length as he looked at her face. "You look well."

"I am well. I thought I'd better come up and say hello before I disappear for six weeks," she said. She threw an arm around his waist as they walked toward the back door of the house, the dog gamboling around them in sheer puppy joy.

"Well, we might actually have some news for you on that score," her father said.

At that moment Shelby's mother, Pauline, came through the door carrying a plate of cheese and biscuits and three glasses.

"Hi, Mum." Shelby walked over and took the glasses and set them down on the table. "What news?"

"Hello, love. We thought we'd go up to Cairns with you on the train. What do you think of that idea?"

Shelby grinned. It was just like them to turn an opportunity into an adventure. "Sounds like a great idea," she said. "I probably won't be able to spend too much time with you on the train, though. I'll have my hands full trying to keep the crew from wreaking havoc when they see the tiny little space they'll be living in for a couple of days."

"That's all right," Ned said as he sat down and started filling his plate. "Just come and say hello every now and then when you can."

Shelby poured a glass of apple juice from the jug on the table. "What are you going to do with yourselves when we get up there?"

"Oh, your mother's got it all planned," he said with a roll of his eyes. "Every silly little museum for a hundred km radius I expect."

Pauline gave him a playful slap across the shoulder. "That's not true, Ned, and you know it." She turned to Shelby. "We're going to go up to Port Douglas and stay for about a week, then rent a car and drive back."

"And we thought we might come and see the show in Cairns," Ned said.

"Great," Shelby replied. "We're going to need all the ticket sales we can get, by the sound of it."

Pauline looked at her. "I thought the show got some really good reviews."

Shelby nodded. "It did. But it's a big city kind of show. I'm not convinced it's going to make much money in outer Woop-Woop, with only half the set and a third of the orchestra." She snaffled a piece of camembert and smeared it onto a cracker.

"They're doing things on the cheap again, are they," Ned asked.

"Eh, it's not that bad," Shelby replied. "They're never going to make money on a country tour—it's just too difficult. So they're trying to lose as little as possible. I don't blame them really. But it does mean a lot more work, and a lot of compromising. What we do have left of the set we're going to have to cut down to make it fit, once we leave Cairns."

"Ugly."

"Just a little bit, yeah. But I guess that's why they pay me the big bucks." Shelby grinned at her father.

"How's Karen?" Pauline asked as she handed Shelby the salad bowl.

Ah. I hate these conversations, Shelby thought. "She can't make the trip," she replied, deliberately misinterpreting the question. "She's got a contract over at the Rep, managing."

"Well, good for her," Pauline said.

Shelby was relieved to get away with such a short conversation. Given the topic of Karen was somewhat fraught anyway, she quickly took the chance to tune into her father's latest adventure in gardening.

"HOW'RE YOU GOING, Tiny?" Shelby asked as she dodged around a stack of black amplifier boxes on the platform. It was 8:15 a.m. the following Monday morning and she already felt that touring a stage show was an over-rated pursuit.

"Good, boss," the stocky Scotsman said. "All my gear's stowed. Want me to help out with something else?"

Shelby glanced down at the clipboard in her hand. On it was a list that seemed to grow longer the more she crossed off it. "Yeah, mate, could you? The sound guys need to get this shit," she kicked at the amplifiers, "onboard. Go find Malcolm and figure out the best place to stow them, yeah?"

"On my way."

"Okay," Shelby muttered. "One down, seven million to go." She made an optimistic mark on the page and ran a finger down the list. "We may get out of here sometime in the next decade..."

"Hello, darling!"

"...unless my mother decides to stop me for a chat." She threw a smile on her face. "Hiya."

Pauline bustled up, all hat and handbag. "I've been looking for you everywhere," she said.

"Been right here, Ma," Shelby replied. "Just been a bit busy."

"Well, I was expecting you to be wearing black, so I missed you." Pauline looked her up down, taking in the casual denim shorts and t-shirt Shelby was wearing. "Why aren't you?"

"Mum, it's not a uniform. We only wear black when we're going to be anywhere near the stage. Otherwise we're actually quite normal."

Pauline reached forward and brushed an errant lock of hair off Shelby's face. "I know that," she said. "Sometimes I just wish you would find a job that was a little more stable."

"Aw, not now, Mum, give me a break." Shelby rolled her eyes at her parental unit. "I'm up to my ass in alligators here, and believe it or not, I'm quite enjoying myself." She grinned, suddenly realizing that for all the annoyance of trying to get the company on the train, that was the truth. "I like my job."

"All right, all right," Pauline said. "Your father and I are up in carriage two, berth twelve. Come and see us when you've settled in."

"I will, Ma." She kissed Pauline on the cheek and watched her weave her way back through the growing scrum of people on the platform. "If she's brought the canasta set I'm in big trouble."

INDEED, CANASTA FEATURED heavily during an evening that was, nonetheless, pleasant for Shelby. She had dinner with the crew back in coach before maneuvering her way up to the sleeper carriage where her parents were berthed. There they whiled away a couple of hours with card games and laughter.

"I give up," Shelby said, finally, throwing down her cards. "I have no idea what I'm doing. I just don't get this game."

"Your mother's cheating," Ned said, as he stood up to stretch. "She always does."

"And your father's lying," Pauline said tartly.

"So, situation normal then?" Shelby laughed.

"Pretty much." Ned began pulling down the bunk bed that hung from the side wall of the small berth. "I suppose you're going to want me to sleep in this thing," he said.

"Well, unless you want me to gripe all night about having to climb up and down, yes," Pauline said. "You know you're much better at that sort of thing than I am."

Shelby decided it was time to vacate the premises. "That's it for me," she said, as she stood up and inched away around her father. "I'm going to give you two some room and head back to the crew quarters." She made her way to the door. "No don't get up, Ma, or we'll all have to breathe in at the same time." She grinned at her parents and blew them a kiss as she backed out of the compartment. "See you tomorrow."

"'Night, love."

"'Night."

Shelby made her way carefully down the swaying carriage. It had generally been a smooth journey to date, although she could feel that the train had sped up considerably in the last hour or so. A night-time thing, I guess, she thought absentmindedly as she pushed herself off one wall.

The sound, when it came, was like nothing Shelby had heard before — metal ripping itself apart, chewing itself up, explosively — but to Shelby it was a physical force, tossing her through the air like a rag doll.

She bounced sickeningly off the end wall of the carriage, only now, she realized in a weird daze of hyper-reality, the carriage was twisting and folding in on itself, toward her. There was screaming, some, she was surprised to find, tearing from her own throat. Some of it didn't sound human at all.

Then everything turned upside down and something hard and unforgiving caught Shelby on her temple and she lost consciousness. She no longer felt the train screeching and grinding to a lurching halt until it lay bleeding, like a wounded, dying snake, its guts spilling over the tracks.

SHE DIDN'T WANT to wake up. It hurt, and it felt like she was trying to breathe underwater. All Shelby wanted was to go back to sleep. But the pain wasn't letting her. Nor was the feeling that she was crushed, enclosed in the tightest of spaces with nowhere to move.

Full consciousness returned with a rush of adrenalin that sent cold shards of terror slicing through her.

"Jesus." What happened? Her panic threatened to bubble over, but she bit down on her bottom lip and tried to think. "Come on, Shelby, think."

She tried to move her arms, and found she could, a little. As far as she could work out she was curled up on her left side. The wall against her back felt solid. So there's no going that way, she realized.

Shelby listened, trying to hear any signs of life around her over the thumping of her heart, but there was an eerie silence, save for the creaking of stressed metal settling and her own breathing.

How long had she been unconscious?

Shelby felt a warm trickling down the side of her face and a quick lick of her lips told her she was tasting blood. She tried moving her legs but a sharp pain and pressure low on her right leg brought her to sudden halt and she let out a hiss of pain.

"Okay. So that's not good." With a grimace she concentrated on her left leg and by raising her hands out in front of her and pushing against the debris she managed to twist it out from under her until she was almost lying on her back.

The pain in her right leg subsided to a manageable level.

"And the good news, Shelby," she muttered to herself, "is that stuff moved when you pushed against it."

She felt her brain starting to function again. If she could somehow gather her strength and lift the wreckage off herself, maybe she could find a way of crawling out of this mess. Maybe then she could go find...the thought of her parents, and the knowledge that whatever had happened, had happened closer to them than to her, gave her a burst of energy that pushed back the claustrophobia and terror.

Knowing her right leg was of no use to her she brought her left knee up to her chest and pushed her foot up against the sheet of metal above her. Then, with a grunt of effort, she shoved up.

Mercifully, the debris moved, showering Shelby in dust and splinters. She pushed up into a sitting position, the relief of being able to breathe and move enough to bring tears to her eyes.

Her right calf was cut from her ankle to just behind her knee, but Shelby was at least glad to see that she wasn't impaled and the bone seemed to be intact. But she was lightheaded and could feel the blood soaking in her jeans.

"Come on. Get out of here."

Shelby looked around. There was nothing recognizable about the train carriage at all. She was indeed resting back against the end wall and above her head were the remains of a window. It took her a few seconds to realize that the carriage, or what was left of it, was on its side. As she looked down the length of the train, back toward where her parents' berth had been, there was nothing but a mess of twisted metal.

Now she could hear human sounds — crying from somewhere quite close to her, what sounded like a child missing her mother. I know how she feels, Shelby thought grimly. Back in that lot are my parents.

That did it. Shelby pushed herself to her feet, tentatively putting weight on her injured leg and finding it hurt, but serviceable.

Carefully she picked her way forward, through the debris, toward the sound of the crying child. She had to stoop and, at one point, crawl over the wreckage but she was rewarded when she found the little girl huddled against the remains of a train seat.

"Hi there," Shelby said, aware that she probably didn't look the most reassuring presence in the world to the scared child. "Are you hurt?"

The girl, who looked to be four or five, shook her head slowly. She was trembling and her dirty face was streaked with tears.

"My name's Shelby. What's yours?"

"Lily."

"Hi, Lily." Shelby started lifting away the rubbish between her and the girl. "How about you and I find a way out of here, hey?"

Lily nodded, but remained where she was, wedged in against the back of the seat. Shelby kept pulling away pieces of debris, but soon came up against something immovable.

"Honey, you're going to have to come toward me, and then I can lift you up and over this," she said. For a moment she feared that the girl wasn't going to move at all, but tentatively the youngster reached out a hand, which Shelby took. "That's it, good girl."

Shelby grunted as she bent her knees, trying to get her legs under her as she lifted the girl out of the little pocket in the debris. The girl was slight, but terrified and she clung to Shelby as if her life depended on it. Shelby felt the thin body shivering in her arms. Shock, she realized. Wonder when that's going to hit me.

"Hey, can anybody in there hear me?" The voice was male and coming from outside the wreckage, Shelby was sure. She looked up at the remains of what was once the side of the carriage, but was now the top of debris.

"Yes, here. Help please," she called out in a voice she barely recognized as her own.

A head appeared above her, outlined against the night sky.

"I'm here," the man said. "Are you hurt? How many of you are there?" Shelby wrapped her arms more tightly around the girl who was clinging to her neck. "Just me and a kid," she said. "We're both okay, I think, but there are plenty of people still in here." She tried not to imagine her parents in the wreck in front of her. "Somewhere."

"Let's get you out, first up," the man said calmly. "More help's coming. There's one ambulance here already and plenty more on the way."

Shelby's eyes adjusted and she could make out the man's features. He was older, with a lined face and kind eyes. He looked like it was an everyday occurrence for him to be pulling people out of train wrecks.

"My name's Bob," he said.

"Shelby," she replied. She tilted her head in the girl's direction. "This is Lily."

"Hello, Lily," Bob said, smiling at the youngster. "Soon have you out of there, kiddo. D'you reckon you can lift her up any higher," he asked Shelby.

"Only one way to find out," Shelby muttered. She felt sick and her head was pounding even harder than her leg was throbbing.

"Okay. Let me get a little closer," Bob said. Shelby watched the man shift himself further over the edge of the debris, reaching down lower toward her.

Shelby moved so she was standing on a slightly higher pile of debris.

"Rightio. On three, okay?"

Shelby shifted the girl's weight in her arms so she could get more purchase. "Lily, I need you to reach up to Bob when I lift you, okay?"

The girl nodded, her eyes wide and almost glazed over with shock.

"One, two...three!"

Shelby hefted the girl skyward, ignoring the pain that screamed in her lower leg as she shifted and stretched. Bob grabbed Lily under her arms and pulled her up and out.

Shelby heard him reassuring her, and then she saw him again, looking down at her, the stars framing his silhouette.

"I'm going to take her down to the paramedics," he said. "Is she yours?"

"No," Shelby said. "I don't know who she belongs to."

"Not to worry. I'll be back soon for you."

Shelby nodded. Without the distraction of having Lily to look out for, she turned her mind to finding her parents. As Bob disappeared with Lily, Shelby climbed back down into the debris and tried to make sense of the tangled metal, glass and other debris. Inch by inch she moved forward, trying to retrace her steps from her parents' berth, struggling to picture how far along the carriage she had moved before chaos erupted.

As she pulled pieces out of the way the noises of the accident began filtering through to her. People were calling to each other, some were clearly in pain. Others were reassuring. Probably rescuers like Bob, she thought.

It took several seconds for Shelby to realize that she was looking at something very familiar. It was a pack of cards, the cover shredded, the individual cards scattered around, some ripped, others crumpled.

Jesus. This was their berth? Shelby stared at the unrecognizable amorphous mass of debris that was the tiny space her parents had been occupying.

"Mum? Dad?" she called out, hoping that somehow they were behind the mess, trapped in a void, just waiting for someone to help them out. There was no response.

Shelby fought down the panic and got down on her knees, scrabbling through the smaller pieces of wreckage, trying to find a way through.

TINY PICKED HIMSELF up off the floor of the carriage. He was surrounded by the rest of the theatre company, all of whom were in various stages of figuring out if they were hurt.

"What the fuck happened?" Phil said, rubbing his elbow as he clambered to his feet.

"Something big, I think, mate," Tiny said grimly. "That sounded like something hit the train. We're not on the tracks anymore, I know that much." Their carriage, though the right way up, was skewed to one side. "Is everyone okay?" he called out.

General assent came from the other occupants and Tony moved over to a window. The train had been rounding a curve and from where they were near the rear of the train, he could see the engine curving away to the left. But between the engine and them, there was chaos.

"Holy shit," Tiny exclaimed. "A truck hit the side of the train! Take a look."

His colleagues rushed to see for themselves and sure enough, the rear end of a semi-trailer protruded from the wreckage, its back wheels in the air. The front end, mangled in the wreckage of the train, was unrecognizable.

"Jesus, Shelby and her parents were up there," Tiny said, looking round to find his other crewmates. "Come on, boys. We've gotta go find them."

The men scrambled out of the train, dropping to the ground and running toward the most damaged portion of the train, where dazed and injured people were already gathering.

SHELBY DIDN'T KNOW how long she sat there, staring at the hand protruding from the debris. She had no concept of the passing of time, nor did she hear anything that was going on around her, anymore. All she knew was that was her mother's hand, the engagement ring she had admired for years in plain view, the watch she had given her mother for her birthday last year still on the wrist.

She also knew the hand was lifeless. Though still warm, there was no pulse and Shelby could see that everything beyond the hand—she closed her eyes against the mental image of her mother's face—was crushed.

There was no sign of her father. If he was still here in the berth then...she couldn't think anymore. Didn't want to think.

Shelby's mind shut down and she hugged her knees to her chest and rocked herself.

Chapter Eleven

Back in Brisbane

EVE SIGHED AND put down her book. She was curled up in the armchair in Shelby's flat, having come down earlier in the evening to feed Rufus and clean out his litter tray. The big black cat had purred at her invitingly from the chair and she'd decided to accept his company.

It was late, at least for Eve, and she reached for the remote control for the small television in the corner, clicking it on in hopes of catching the headlines on the late news before she called it a night.

The familiar face of the news anchorman flickered to life and Eve had to smile. His wife was one of her clients, and she knew more about the perfectly manicured talking head than she really wanted to know. "If his bosses knew what he gets up to out of hours, Rufus." she muttered as she scratched the cat behind his ears. "Oh, who am I kidding? They probably wouldn't give a damn as long as he turned up on time for work."

She put aside her prejudices against the man and tried to concentrate on what he was saying as a graphic appeared over his right shoulder showing a mangled pile of wreckage and the words "twenty-three dead."

"Emergency services are at the scene of a major train accident just north of Rockhampton this evening," the anchorman said. Eve felt a sudden surge of cold, deep in her gut. "Although the details of exactly what happened are yet to emerge, it seems a semi-trailer collided at high speed with the northbound Sundowner Express at about 9:15 p.m. Police have confirmed that twenty-three bodies, including the driver of the truck, have so far been pulled from the wreckage. Some passengers remain trapped and fire rescue teams are using the jaws of life to attempt to reach them. More from Jenny Rogers, on the scene."

"Oh my god." Eve jumped up, startling Rufus and sending him scurrying from the room. "Jesus, Shelby." Nothing in the journalist's report told her anything she wanted to know — where Shelby was, whether or not she was hurt. For a full minute Eve's mind was frozen in shock.

The news bulletin moved on to the next item and Eve turned off the television, tossing the remote control into the chair as she moved back toward the stairs that led to her part of the house. She passed Shelby's telephone on the way and suddenly the obvious occurred.

"Call her cell phone. Of course." Eve reached for the phone and dialed Shelby's number from memory. It rang and rang and just as Eve was about to hang up, a familiar, but scared voice answered.

"E-Eve?"

"Oh, thank god...Shelby...are you all right?"

"I...I'm not sure...I think so...cuts and bruises, I think..."

"Your parents?" Eve heard Shelby swallowing hard, clearly overwhelmed. "Shelby?"

"I don't know where Dad is...Mum...I think she's...she's..."

Eve closed her eyes against the pain she could hear in Shelby's voice. "Oh, honey...Shelby, where are you?"

"Ambulance." Shelby's voice sounded drowsy and more disconnected.

"Where are they taking you?" Shelby said nothing and Eve wondered for a moment if the line had dropped out. "Shelby?"

"Uh, hello, this is Gary Schaeffer, I'm the paramedic..."

"Oh, is she okay? Where are you taking her?"

"Rockhampton General, ma'am... and apart from a couple of nasty lacerations I think there's also a bad concussion there, maybe other internal injuries."

"Thank you. Please, if you get a chance, tell her Eve is on the way."

"Yes, ma'am."

Eve hung up. She could feel her brain starting to work now that the shock was subsiding. "Call Karen, get dressed, pick her up, drive to Rockhampton. Okay, Eve, come on, get moving."

She picked up Shelby's address book from where it lay next to the phone and flipped through the pages until she found Karen's number. Her mind was already racing ahead as she waited for the phone to answer. It was incongruous to hear a party going on in the background.

"Karen?"

"Yeah, who's this?"

"It's Eve Morgan... Shelby's, uh...housemate. I'm afraid I've got some bad news."

"Hang on, let me get somewhere quiet." There was a pause and muffled noises as the sounds of the party faded a little. "What's up, Dr. Morgan?"

"There's been an accident...the train Shelby and her parents and the theatre company were on...well, there was a crash. Shelby's okay," she said hastily, hearing a catch in Karen's breathing. "But she's in hospital in Rockhampton. I'm not really sure about her parents. From her reaction it sounded like something very bad has happened to her mother and her father is missing."

"Wow...I'm, uh, glad she's okay," said Karen quietly.

"Well, like I said, it's relative," Eve replied. "Look, where are you? I'll come pick you up and we'll get moving."

"Um, that's pretty heavy...her parents are dead?"

Eve felt a certain impatience but kept her temper in check, knowing Karen would be as shocked as she had been. "From what she said, she saw her mother and, well...she didn't exactly say, but that's what I got reading between the lines. Where are you?"

"Um, look...I can't do that."

"What do you mean? Can't do what?"

"I can't go up there and see her. I...uh...I don't do hospitals."

Eve felt a gear slipping in her head. "You don't do — Karen, you're kidding, right? She's hurt and she's going to need her friends — especially you."

"I can't, okay? Just...tell her I'm glad she's all right."

"For God's sake, Karen..." Eve was at a loss for words.

"Look, Eve...I can't. I just can't." Karen sounded angry and defensive and Eve half-expected her to hang up.

"Okay, okay," she said. "Could you at least come over and feed the cat? I don't know how long she's going to be in hospital, or how soon I can get her back down here."

For a moment she thought Karen would even refuse to help that much, but then she heard a sigh.

"Yeah...sure...yeah, I can do that. Where does Shelby keep the key?"

Eve breathed out slowly. "In the flowerpot by the front door, under the stone. Thank you for doing that."

"It's the least I can do," Karen said.

"Boy, you got that right," Eve said and hung up, beyond caring about the woman's feelings at that point. "I'll be damned."

Rufus brought her out of her thoughts by weaving around her legs. "Something tells me I should put down some extra food and water for you just in case, boycat," she said to the feline. She reached down and scratched between his ears. "Don't worry, Rufus, I'll bring your mama home as soon as I can."

IT WAS MIDNIGHT before Eve finally hit the road to Rockhampton. She'd gathered together a few changes of clothes for herself, packed clothes and toiletries for Shelby, left a message for her receptionist to cancel her appointments for the week and finally locked the house up.

Now it was just about dawn as she pulled into the parking lot of the small general hospital. For the hour, it was surprisingly busy as she walked into the reception area. Police, nurses, and civilians were milling about, some waiting just outside the emergency room doors, others snatching what sleep they could in the armchairs in the middle of the big lobby. Eve intercepted a nurse carrying an important looking clipboard.

"Hello, can you help me? I'm looking for...she was in the train crash...Shelby Macrossan?"

The nurse looked at her kindly. "Are you a member of her family?" she asked.

Eve hesitated, torn between lying and the risk of not being allowed to see Shelby. "I'm her housemate—and right now, there's a good possibility that her family were killed in the crash...I really need to see her."

"Your name, please?"

Eve decided to use her title. It wasn't a lie, but it was leverage she badly needed. "Dr. Eve Morgan."

The nurse's attitude changed immediately and she looked down the list of names on her clipboard. "Ah, yes, here she is. Before you go and see her, could I ask that you register with the counseling team we've got on hand? We're trying to keep track of who has friends and family available and who we still have to contact. We've set up a room for relatives of people in the crash...if you go there first, you'll find police officers and counselors who will be able to give you more information. Once you're done there, we'll be able to let you see her."

Eve nodded, more familiar than the nurse knew about these kinds of situations. "Thank you, I certainly will do that, but first, can you tell me about Shelby's injuries?"

The nurse looked down at her notes again. "She has a pretty nasty concussion—we've been waking her every couple of hours and she's doing a lot better than when she was first admitted...also she has a deep laceration on her scalp that required fifteen stitches, and another on her right calf that needed forty-two. Other than that she's covered in bruises and small scratches, but there's no sign at this stage of any internal bleeding."

Eve let out the breath she hadn't realized she'd been holding. "So there's a decent chance you can discharge her soon?"

The nurse nodded. "Probably by the end of the day if she keeps improving like she has been through the night. But she'll need to stay quiet for a few days, and of course, she'll need crutches for a while."

"Thank you so much," Eve said gratefully.

Further down the hall she found the makeshift crisis room. There was a tired-looking policewoman compiling lists in one corner, talking on the phone. Other people, clearly friends and relatives of those involved in the crash, were sitting around the room looking dazed. Several women, obviously counselors, were sitting with them or circulating around the room.

The policewoman finished her phone conversation and Eve headed in her direction.

"Can I help you, ma'am?"

"I hope so, officer," Eve replied. "I have a friend, Shelby Macrossan, who was in the train wreck—she's been admitted here and I know she's doing okay, but I need to know about her parents—they were traveling with her."

"You're a friend?"

Eve suppressed a sigh, knowing that the policewoman was just doing her job. "Yes. I'm also her housemate and I...used to be her therapist." She pulled out her purse and dug out a business card which she handed to the constable as proof of her credentials.

The policewoman nodded. "Fair enough, Dr....uh...Morgan. What are her parents' names?"

Eve sat down across the table. "Pauline and Ned Macrossan."

The cop's finger traced down the passenger list, and Eve held her breath, hoping against hope that a little miracle had happened.

"Here they are." The policewoman sighed and looked up. "I'm sorry. They're both deceased. They were brought into the morgue earlier this morning. They had ID on them."

Eve closed her eyes, already empathizing with what Shelby would be feeling. "Damn." She opened her eyes again and looked directly at the young officer. "Do you know if Shelby knows yet?"

"It's unlikely," the policewoman said. "We're still in the process of cross-checking the lists of the dead and the injured, so if your friend came in by ambulance and was admitted straight away, we wouldn't have had a chance to link her to her parents, let alone tell her."

Eve looked down at her hands, crossed in her lap. She knew it was going to be up to her.

"Do you want someone to come with you?" the policewoman asked gently.

Eve shook her head quickly, chasing away the sudden tears. "No. No, thank you, officer."

The policewoman handed her a card. "Here's the number of the funeral home that's organizing the transportation of the bodies."

Eve nodded numbly. "Thanks."

A counselor who had overheard the last part of the conversation came up and touched Eve on the shoulder.

"Is there anything I can do?" she asked. "Come with you to see your friend, maybe?"

Eve stood up and smiled wanly at the woman. "Thanks for the thought. But I'll be okay with it. In theory, this is what I do for a living."

The counselor nodded. "You're Eve Morgan."

"Yes...how did you—?"

"I was at a conference last year where you gave a paper on grieving."

"Ah." It figures. Small world.

"You said...in theory?"

Eve nodded. "Yes. Shelby's a good friend, and her parents...I knew them. This isn't going to be very pleasant."

"Might be easier if I did the hard part for you."

Eve thought about it. It was certainly a tempting offer. "No. I think it would be better coming from me. Thank you, though." She looked around at the rest of the room. "You look like you have a long day ahead of you."

"Oh yeah," the other woman replied. "The families are only just starting to arrive."

"Good luck," Eve said.

"Thanks."

THE NURSE OPENED the door and stood aside to let Eve past. "I just did the six a.m. obs," the young woman said. "So she gets to sleep for another few hours at least." Eve nodded, unable to take her eyes off the pale figure in the bed.

Shelby looked so young lying there, sleep taking all the tension out of her face. Her dark hair was splayed across the pillow, and her fringe was plastered to her forehead with perspiration. There was a bandage over her left temple back to behind her ear, and Eve noted, there was a cage over Shelby's right leg, presumably where she had suffered the other laceration.

"Oh, honey," Eve whispered.

There was a smear of dried blood on Shelby's left cheek. Eve pulled a tissue from the box on the bedside stand and dipped a corner of it in to the jug of cold water that stood next to it. Carefully she wiped away the blood, watching Shelby's eyes twitching behind their lids.

Eve gently picked up Shelby's left hand and squeezed it, trying to restore some warmth to its cool clamminess.

"H'lo."

"You're supposed to be asleep, sweetheart." Eve smiled as she watched Shelby try to open her eyes, without much success.

"M'a bit loopy," Shelby muttered, her brow creased in concentration.

"Mhm. I expect you're full of painkillers," Eve replied, as she brushed the hair from Shelby's forehead, smoothing away the creases with her thumb.

"S'nice. Don't stop doing that."

"You need to sleep." *I don't want to tell you what I have to tell you yet.*

"Can't."

"Why not?"

"Have to tell you something."

"It can wait, Shelby."

"Nope. Can't."

"Okay." Eve waited, half-thinking that Shelby had fallen back asleep again. "Shelby?"

"M'here. I think."

Eve chuckled softly. "Honey, whatever it is, tell me when you wake up, okay?"

"Nope. S'important. Just gotta remember what it is."

"Shelby..."

"I love you."

Ah.

"'N' you're not allowed to say somethin' therapistish like 'that's nice', either. M'sick, don't forget."

Eve smiled, charmed by the childlike pout on Shelby's face, even though she still hadn't opened her eyes. Still holding Shelby's hand, she leaned down until her mouth was next to Shelby's ear.

"Shelby, I'm not your therapist anymore. And I love you too." Then she pulled back a little and placed a gentle kiss on Shelby's forehead.

"I knew that." Shelby's face relaxed as she drifted back toward sleep. "Don't go 'way?"

"I'm not going anywhere, sweetheart," Eve murmured, sitting down in the chair beside the bed. "Sleep now."

LONG DAY, EVE thought as she stared out of the window of Shelby's hospital room. She had spent the day dealing with a succession of visitors while Shelby continued to sleep fitfully. There had been no chance to tell her about her parents.

Between the members of the theatre company, including the general manager who had driven up to take control and check on his favorite employee, and the police and the counselors, not to mention the regular drop-ins from nurses and doctors, there had been barely a moment to think.

"E-Eve?"

Quickly she moved back to Shelby's side and took her hand. "Yes, honey, I'm here."

"W-what happened?" For the first time Shelby's eyes looked clear and drug-free, and her disorientation was obvious. "Where are we?"

"We're in the hospital in Rockhampton," Eve replied. "You were hurt in a..."

Shelby's eyes widened. "Oh my god, the train."

She surged up from the bed, trying to sit up, threatening to rip the IV line from her right hand. Eve tried to press her back down gently.

"Easy, sweetheart. Just lie back. You've got a bit of a concussion. Don't rush things."

Shelby grabbed Eve's hand desperately.

"M-my parents...where are they? Are they all right?"

Eve took a deep breath. "Honey, I need you to lie back...I'm afraid I've got some bad news to tell you."

Shelby's hand gripped her harder as a memory clicked back into place. "My mother...oh my god...Eve, I remember...my mother."

"They're both dead, Shelby," Eve said, knowing it was best just to say it. "I'm so sorry."

She waited, trying to read the emotions visible on Shelby's face. Shelby was trying to piece things together in her head, she knew. Connecting the reality of what she had seen and experienced with the words Eve had just said.

"Both of them?" Eve nodded. "But, I couldn't find Dad. Maybe he just wandered away or something. Didn't know where he was. And they just haven't found him yet?" Hopeful brown eyes locked with Eve's.

"No, hon, I'm sorry. They found them both. Your father was...he was thrown clear of the wreckage on impact, but he didn't survive. They've identified them both."

Shelby moaned softly and Eve wrapped her arms around her, letting Shelby lean forward against her chest, the dark head tucked under Eve's chin. She slowly stroked Shelby's hair.

"I'm so sorry, sweetheart."

Shelby didn't cry. She wasn't there yet, Eve knew. "Honey, there's nothing you need to do now except rest and heal," Eve said, as if reading her mind.

"Easier said than done," she mumbled into Eve's neck.

"I know, baby. Just trust me for now, and get some more sleep. Things will happen as and when they have to."

"Can I sleep here?" Shelby whispered. Eve smiled to herself, feeling Shelby relaxing into her arms. "Don't you think you'd be more comfortable lying down?"

There was no reply and Eve gently lowered Shelby back on to the bed, unwinding her arms from around the sleeping woman. She looked down at her, noting the crease in her forehead, despite the sleep that had already taken her over.

"Best thing you can do right now, love," she said. "What a day."

Chapter Twelve

THE NEXT MORNING Eve and Shelby were driving south again. The doctors had reluctantly released Shelby into Eve's care, Shelby refusing the medical advice to have another night in the hospital. She just wanted to get home and begin making whatever arrangements needed to be done.

Eve was glad to be on the road and doing something. The atmosphere at the hospital had been grim—with the death toll from the crash now over thirty and the small facility full of anxious and grieving family members.

So far the drive had been very quiet. Shelby was still taking some strong painkillers and she was lying back in the reclined passenger seat, giving her injured leg some room to stretch out. Eve concentrated on the road in front of them, making lists in her head of things that needed doing once they reached Shelby's parental home, their first port of call.

"Why didn't Karen come?" Shelby asked, out of the blue.

Eve sighed. Shelby had been inundated with bad news in the past twenty-four hours; this was something else she didn't need. But there was no point in lying.

"She said she couldn't," Eve replied.

"She didn't want to."

"I don't know, Shelby...she just said she couldn't."

"I guess that's that then."

Privately Eve agreed. Karen is young and doesn't want the complications of this kind of commitment...but what's the point of saying that now. "I think you need to let that be for now."

They fell back into silence as another few kilometers slipped by.

"What happens now? I mean, there must be things I need to organize." Shelby reached up and touched the small bandage at her temple. Eve noted the vague, unfocused expression on her face

"They're all in hand. I've been making phone calls for you," Eve said.

"Where are...where are their...where are my parents?"

"On the way back home...the funeral director picked them up last night."

"I...I have power of attorney...I need to contact my parents' lawyers."

"Mhm...we can do that as soon as we get home."
"I need to pick up Pip."
Eve was baffled by that one. "Who's Pip?"
"Um...their dog...Labrador...he's at a kennel...somewhere," Shelby replied. She turned to look at Eve. "How do you feel about having a dog around the house—I don't think I can stand the thought of...he's very sweet."
Eve smiled. This part at least is easy. "I think that's a great idea...how do you think Rufus will take to it?'
"He'll just have to get used to it." Shelby looked at Eve again. "Thank you."
"It'll be great to have a dog around the place again."
"I didn't just mean about the dog."
"I know...it's okay, Shelby. Let's just get you through the next few days."

EVE WALKED THROUGH the house carrying a tray of hors d'oeuvres. As she moved from room to room she offered the food to the many mourners who had come back to Ned and Pauline's house after the funeral. The couple had been popular, long-standing members of their community and people had come from near and far to pay their respects.

Shelby had been a force of nature over the past week. Once they arrived at her parents' home she had occupied herself with the long list of arrangements and meetings with lawyers that her parents' death had necessitated.

Eve helped out when needed, but mostly she had kept a weather eye on Shelby, knowing full well that it was shock and adrenalin keeping her on her feet and moving forward, despite being on crutches and very sore. She had a fair inkling that as the house emptied and the long list of chores came to an end Shelby would feel the full force of the loss of her parents. And it's going to suck mightily, Eve thought.

For now, though, Shelby was firing on all cylinders, mingling with her parents' friends, comforting them and sharing happy memories. Pip, the Labrador, was following her around the house, sitting patiently by her side as she talked and played the hostess.

Eve took the half-empty tray back into the kitchen and placed it down on the counter-top. She was tired, there was no denying. She had shuttled between here and her place a couple of times, picking up Rufus and bringing him here, rather than leaving him to the dubious and unreliable care of Karen. The big black cat was disgruntled by being out of his environment and in the same space as a boisterous puppy and had taken to hiding under the bed in one of the spare rooms. Ah well, he'll get used to it, Eve thought as she reloaded the tray with fresh food.

SHELBY SHOOK THE hand of her father's best friend, Harry James, as he and his wife stood at the front door, on their way home after the wake.

"Thanks for coming, Harry," she said, with a smile. "I know Dad would have appreciated it."

"Can't believe the old bugger's gone," Harry said, shaking his head sadly. "I only saw him last weekend. We played a round of golf."

"Who won?" Shelby asked, trying to jolly her old family friend into a smile.

"He did, of course," Harry said, rewarding her with a grin. "He never did concede a thing. Competitive bastard."

"Yeah, that's Dad for you," she said.

"We'll see you around, Shelby," Harry said. "If there's anything you need, don't hesitate to give us a call, okay?"

"Thanks, will do," she said. Right now all she wanted was to get people on their way home so she could get a little peace and quiet. But it was hard to rush folk who were being so kind and complimentary about her parents. She had been amazed at the offers of help and advice that had come her way since news of the accident had spread around the small country town.

Shelby felt a familiar presence at her elbow and she looked around to see Eve close by. "Hi."

"Hello."

"Feeling the need to send these people home," Shelby said, answering the unasked question.

Eve nodded. "Mhm. Enough's enough, hey?"

"Oh yeah."

"Leave it to me. Why don't you retreat to the bedroom for a while?"

Shelby considered that thought for a moment. "Good idea. Do you think people will notice?"

"They'll understand. And if you're not visible, they'll stop feeling the need to tell you how they're feeling."

Shelby chuckled. "You say that from experience, I take it?"

"Oh yeah. Give people the opportunity to offer their sympathies and they'll do it for hours on end." Eve patted her on the shoulder. "Go on. While they're all distracted."

Shelby nodded. "Thanks, Eve. I feel bad leaving you with this lot, though."

"Don't. By the time you emerge I'll have persuaded them to do the washing-up and cleaning before they go." She smiled at Shelby, noting the dark circles that had formed under her eyes. "Go clear your head. Take a nap or listen to some music."

"Okay." Shelby tucked the crutches under her arms and hobbled back in to the house, Pip in tow.

EVE BLINKED IN the darkness, wondering what it was that had roused her from a deep sleep. If she didn't know better she would have said it was a cold, wet puppy nose. It took a few seconds for her eyes to adjust and then, there it was. A black, shiny Labrador snout, inches from her face.

"Pip, what's up?" she muttered, wondering what could have shifted the dog from his prized spot on the bottom corner of Shelby's bed. A wagging tail was the only response she received, however. Eve reached out and patted the soft head, scratching behind the floppy ears for good measure. "You can't be hungry...oh wait, you're a Labrador, of course you are."

A glance at the digital clock on the nightstand of the guest bedroom she was occupying told her it was just after 3 a.m. Ugh. "Seriously, pooch, what's wrong?" Eve sat up and rubbed her eyes. "Has Shelby gone wandering again, hmmm?" She knew Shelby hadn't been sleeping all that well since the accident, but the dog didn't usually feel compelled to come and tell Eve about it. "Okay, okay, I'm getting up."

She swung her legs over the side of the bed and grabbed the dressing gown she had left on the foot of the bed. Pulling it on she stood and walked out into the hallway. She could see that a light was on in the living room and she made her way toward it.

Shelby was sitting on the floor, her back against the couch. She was surrounded by piles of papers and boxes and she was absorbed in the handful of photographs she was flipping through.

Eve leaned up against the doorjamb and watched Shelby for a few seconds.

"Hi," she finally said.

Pip walked past Eve and rejoined his new best friend, slumping down at Shelby's side as she looked up at Eve.

"Sorry, did I wake you?"

Eve shook her head and pushed herself off the doorjamb. She walked over to the armchair and slumped down into it. "Nope. Your furry friend came and snuffled me. I figured he thought you need some company."

Shelby looked apologetic. "Tch, silly bugger. There's no

reason you shouldn't sleep just because I can't, Eve."

Eve watched as Shelby's head bent to look at the photographs again. She knew exactly what was going on with Shelby, understood it totally and knew what she would be doing if she was Shelby's counselor. Which I'm not, she reminded herself for about the millionth time since the train crash. "It's okay. It's not like there's been a lot of time to talk since we got home." Since your parents were killed in a horrific crash that you were also in, that hurt you physically and saw you witness things nobody should see, her mind completed the unspoken part of the sentence. Come on, Shelby. You know this is something you have to deal with, one way or another, with or without my help.

Shelby was staring at one particular photo. "This is Mum and Dad on their thirty-fifth wedding anniversary. I took it when they were cutting the cake. They look happy with each other," she murmured.

Eve nodded, letting Shelby go where she needed to go.

"I'm glad they were together," Shelby said. "God knows they did everything else together. It makes sense they would die together as well." She looked up at Eve again. "Are you as weirded out by this as I am?" she asked.

Eve smiled. "Depends what you mean by weirded out," she replied. "I am feeling a little off-balance, but then it's not really surprising. I'm tired and I'm concerned about you."

"You've been looking after me so well," Shelby said. "Thank you for everything."

Eve shrugged. "You'd do the same for me," she said. "In fact, you did, as I recall."

"Mmmm, no, not like this. I just turned up at the right moment. You were here for me from the word go."

"Shelby."

She looked up, catching Eve's eye. "Yes?"

"Do you want to talk about it?"

"You mean, client to therapist?"

Eve sighed. It was a very familiar conversation. Shelby was deflecting left, right and backwards, talking in circles trying to find as many ways as possible of avoiding the heart of the matter. Fourteen years of therapy and four years of friendship had taught Eve that much.

"No," she said. "If you want to talk to a therapist, then by all means, I'll recommend someone for you. But I think if you look around you'll notice that I don't sit in my dressing gown at 3 a.m. for many of my clients. None of them, in fact."

Shelby's eyes dropped again. "I know."

There's only one way to crack this nut, Eve decided. Gonna have to make it clear that it's her friend here, not some professional counselor. Otherwise we'll be dancing around this for hours, if not days.

She stood and walked over to Shelby. Shelby looked up at her as she stood next to her, then Eve gathered her dressing gown and plonked herself down on the carpet next to Shelby. She sat close enough that their shoulders were touching. She heard Shelby breathe out slowly.

"Can I have a look at some these photographs?" she asked gently.

"Sure," Shelby replied, handing them over. "Mum and Dad weren't terribly organized with their pictures. There's not an album in sight. Just piles of pics with captions written on the back. Some of them don't even make sense."

"That might be a good project," Eve said. "Sort them out into a kind of history."

Shelby nodded and picked up another pile of papers. She leaned against Eve, who felt Shelby relax a little more.

"These are letters they sent each other," Shelby said, turning the papers over in her hand. "Oh wow," she muttered.

"What?"

"These are from when they were courting," Shelby said. "Love letters." Hastily she gathered the rest of them up and bundled them together with a convenient elastic band. "Well, I'm not going to be reading those," she said.

"Why not?" Eve asked. "Do you really think they would mind?"

"Apart from the fact they're dead, you mean?" Shelby quipped, then stopped short. "Ugh. That's not funny."

Eve tilted her head, watching Shelby closely. "No, but it's where you're at right now, so don't worry about it." She took the letters from Shelby and put them to one side. "You know, these letters might give you a really interesting insight into their relationship. It might be a good way to remember them."

Shelby looked sharply at her. "D'you really think I'm going to forget them?" She looked defensive, and confused.

Easy, Eve told herself. Right on the brink here. "No, I don't. Not for a minute. But there's nothing wrong with finding different ways of thinking about them."

Shelby crossed her arms and rested her chin on her chest, deep in thought. "But, see, that's the thing, Eve. I don't want to think about them. I don't actually feel anything right now. It's like it's all happening to some other family."

"Mhm, I know." Shelby's body language was a mess of

mixed messages, Eve realized. On the one hand she was relaxed and leaning against Eve. On the other she was closing herself off and not meeting her eyes. The body reflecting the mind, as always, Eve thought. She doesn't know what to feel right now. "Tell me something?"

"Mmmm?"

"You're not sleeping much, right?"

Shelby rubbed her eyes. "Nope."

"Is that because you've tried and can't? Or because you don't want to try?" Eve didn't give Shelby a chance to fold her arms again, instead taking her right hand in her own left and squeezing it gently, holding it as they rested on Shelby's thigh. She was encouraged when Shelby squeezed back.

"Good question...as always," Shelby said, smiling slightly. "Since the hospital I've been avoiding sleep, honestly."

"Too many pictures in your head?"

Shelby nodded slowly.

"I can't remember much about being in hospital. Just...nightmares."

"Tell me about them?" Eve said softly.

Shelby dropped her head back and rested it on the couch cushion. "God, Eve, trust me, you don't want to know."

Eve nudged her with her shoulder. "I wouldn't have asked if I didn't think it was important to get it outside yourself, honey."

There was a long pause as Shelby looked at the ceiling and tried to find the words.

"I...I was really glad I didn't have to see...them...afterwards...if you know what I mean. That I didn't have to identify them." A thought suddenly occurred to her and she sat up straight quickly. "Oh, god, Eve, you didn't have to, did you?"

Eve shook her head. "No. The police said it wasn't necessary. Your father..." She hesitated and Shelby tugged her hand.

"Go on, it's okay," she said, a little hoarsely.

"Well, he still had his wallet on him. So they had his driver's license. I don't really know how they identified your mother."

"I do," Shelby said, her eyes glazed over by the thought. "I was right there when they...when they pulled her out." She shook her head against the onslaught of pictures in her mind. "Remember I told you about the little girl and the man who took her out for me?"

Eve nodded. They had found out that Lily had been reunited with her parents, who had been only slightly hurt in the train wreck.

"He came back for me and when he saw...that I had found my mother, he got a lot of firemen to come and pull her out."

Eve watched as Shelby grew very pale as she recounted the details of the crews cutting her mother's body from the wreckage.

"They tried to make me go outside and not watch...but...Jesus, Eve." She turned wide brown eyes on Eve. "What the hell was I thinking? And why am I only remembering this now?"

"Because it's safe for you to remember it now," Eve said. "You've had a lot to do since we got back. The funeral arrangements, the wake, the wills, the attorneys, putting this place on the market. For goodness sake, Shelby, you delivered the eulogy yourself."

"It was good, too," Shelby said offhandedly.

"Yes, it was," Eve said, letting the moment of humor cut the tension a little. "I was very proud of you. You made people laugh at a funeral, for crying out loud."

"Yeah, well, I'm a funny girl."

Eve chuckled. Always with the jokes. "The point is," she continued, refocusing the conversation, "if you'd let those memories resurface before now, you wouldn't have been able to do all the things you felt you needed to do."

Shelby gazed at her, and suddenly Eve was aware of how close they were, their faces inches apart.

"And now I'm safe," Shelby whispered.

"And now you're safe." Eve cleared her throat of the frog that had appeared from nowhere. "As for what you were thinking in the middle of all that horror, my best guess would be that you needed to know for sure."

Shelby nodded, still staring at Eve. "I knew it was her hand...I mean...her hand was..." She swallowed and Eve squeezed her fingers again. "All I could see was her hand. The rest of her was buried. But the fireman said I didn't want to see her like this. And he was right, I didn't...but..."

"But, you had to," Eve finished for her. Shelby nodded again. "Do you want to tell me more?"

Now the words came pouring out of Shelby. "There was a lot of blood," she said. "Her legs and body were just...ruined." She looked at Eve, searching for the right words. "Ruined. But when they got to her...her face...It was just like she was asleep," she said. "I was so glad about that."

Eve felt her own tears pricking and saw Shelby's eyes welling up. Good girl, she thought. "Let it out, sweetheart," she whispered, encouraging.

"But then they tried to move her. And she just...she kind of..." She looked desperate now, and Eve felt herself wanting to hold Shelby, comfort her any way she could. "Eve, she just...fell apart." The last two words came out in a hoarse wail that pierced Eve's heart like a knife. She gave in to her instincts and wrapped Shelby in a close hug.

Shelby dissolved into long, hitching sobs that had been days in the making. Shelby's head was tucked under Eve's chin and Eve found herself rocking them both back and forth gently.

"That's it, baby, just let it out," she crooned against Shelby's hair. "I'm so sorry you had to see that. Nobody should have to see that." Silently she cursed the rescue crews for not bodily removing Shelby from the site, mother or no mother. And then she remembered that it was no bed of roses for them either.

Shelby was lost in hurt as Eve held her close. The pain poured up and out of her like it was welling up from some bottomless pit. Each sob sounded as though it would never end.

The dog woke from where he had slumbered against Shelby's side and sat up to provide his own brand of support, placing a paw on her arm, his head tilted to one side in a look of canine concern.

It was enough to break the cycle and Shelby choked out a teary laugh. She reached out a hand and patted Pip even as she relaxed against Eve's chest. "Good dog."

Eve pulled them both back against the couch until they were completely relaxed. She didn't want to let Shelby go while she was still so open and vulnerable.

"You know what I think?" she said quietly.

"What?" Shelby asked between sobs that were becoming less violent and more soulful.

"I think your mother would be very glad that you were there to make sure she was taken care of at that moment."

"I wasn't there at the important moment, though, was I?" Shelby said bleakly. "If I'd been with them when that goddamn truck hit, then..."

"...then you'd be dead too, Shelby, and that would be..." Eve sought the right word. "Unthinkable." She shivered.

Shelby stayed still and quiet, snuggled in as she was, her face against the soft skin of Eve's neck. "I scared the crap out of you, huh?" Shelby said quietly.

"You have no idea," Eve said. "Until I heard your voice on the phone I was running around in circles like a headless chook."

Shelby wrapped her arms around Eve's waist and snuggled in even closer. "I don't believe that for a second. You've never been flustered."

"You've never seen me flustered. There's a big difference," Eve replied, happy to take part in the more lighthearted conversation.

And then she felt Shelby's lips brush against her neck.

Oh, Shelby, she thought. Your timing. "You're about to see me flustered, if you keep doing that," she said out loud, trying to keep her voice casual.

Shelby tilted her head back and kissed the soft spot just below Eve's ear, nuzzling. Eve groaned softly.

"Shelby," Eve pleaded. The unexpected sensations were...god, wonderful...but...but what, Eve? You know you want this. You've wanted it for months.

Shelby wasn't to be diverted as she trailed a line of kisses along the line of Eve's jaw.

Got to stop this, Eve thought, even as she found her fingers tracing slow circles in the small of Shelby's back. "Shelby...honey...please stop."

"Don't want to," came the response between kisses as Shelby lifted herself up and leaned in, intent on switching her attentions to Eve's lips. Instead she met an earnest pair of blue eyes and a gentle pair of fingers pressed against her mouth.

"And believe me, I very much wish you didn't have to," Eve said, with a sigh. "But you do have to."

The crestfallen look on Shelby's face almost broke Eve's heart. "Did I...god, Eve, I'm sorry..." Eve grabbed Shelby's hand as she scrambled to climb out of her lap.

"Don't. Don't run away from me this time, please," Eve pleaded, tugging her back so she could keep her close. "You haven't done anything wrong."

"Then...then why?"

Eve reached up and brushed a stray lock of auburn hair from Shelby's eyes with her fingertip.

"Awful timing, sweetheart," she said. "Think about it."

Shelby groaned and buried her face against Eve's shoulder. "I don't want to."

That provoked a chuckle. "Exactly." She planted a soft kiss in Shelby's hair and wrapped her arms around her once again. "Do you really want us to start this way, when you have so much on your plate?" Shelby's sigh gave her the answer. "One huge emotional jolt at a time, hey?"

Shelby nodded, and settled back into her comfortable spot tucked under Eve's chin, wrapped up in strong, safe arms. Her eyes closed and a warm lassitude swept over her. "Did I at least fluster you?" she murmured.

"Oh yes. Thoroughly," Eve replied, the smile evident in her voice. "Do you think you can sleep now, honey?" Her answer came in the tiniest of nods and a deep sigh as the woman in her arms drifted away. That's it, sweetheart. Sleep deep.

Chapter Thirteen

Three weeks later

SHELBY OPENED THE door of her apartment for the first time in three weeks and stood for a moment on the threshold. Everything was just as she'd left it, but so much had happened since then that it all felt a little...disconcerting, somehow. She tossed her keys on to the table by the door and hefted her bag from one hand to the other as she walked inside. There was a friendly meow from her left and she turned to find Rufus sauntering toward her, tail high.

"Hello, old mate," she said as she put down her bag and sat cross-legged on the floor by the cat. He happily clambered into her lap and proceeded to purr loudly. "It's good to see you too." Eve had brought Rufus and Pip down from her parents' place two weeks earlier when she had decided she needed to get back to work. It had given Shelby a chance to concentrate on clearing up her parents' affairs and getting the house and furniture sold.

She had put most of her mother and father's personal effects into storage, along with some pieces of furniture that she couldn't bear to part with, but for the most part it had been a better solution to put most of it on the market. She hadn't felt particularly attached to the house, as her folks had moved there after she graduated college, so that hadn't been a huge wrench.

But it was good to be back in her own space.

There was a knock on the door between her apartment and the main part of the house.

"Come on in," Shelby called out.

Eve opened the door and grinned at Shelby. "I thought I heard your car pull in," she said. "Welcome home." She left the door open and walked down the steps.

"Thanks," Shelby said. "How are you?" She hadn't seen Eve since a couple of days after the funeral and they had talked only a few times on the phone.

"Pretty good, thanks," said Eve. "Any minute now, we're going to be invaded when Pip realizes I'm not where he left me." She grinned.

There was a silence as both women listened for the sound of puppy feet. Sure enough, within a few seconds the Labrador burst in, all paws and ears, barreling down the steps toward Shelby. Rufus dashed for the safety of Shelby's bedroom, and she caught the dog full in the chest.

"Oof, Jesus. Hello, Pip, you lunatic," Shelby gasped as Eve laughed. "Yes, I missed you too, fella." She endured a lavish Labrador licking before pushing the dog away. "He's settled in, then?" she asked.

"Oh yes," Eve said as she took a seat in the nearest armchair. "He and Rufus even get along fairly well as long as he doesn't try and sneak up on the cat. That usually ends in tears for someone."

Pip had now rolled on his back, offering his belly for a good scratching, which Shelby duly provided.

"What's new with you?" she asked Eve.

"Not much. Got back to work and it was like I'd never had a week off. Crises from breakfast to bedtime."

"Wonderful. But I know that's what you love about it." She looked at Eve and met her eyes. There was a gentle kind of tension between them that was by no means unpleasant. They hadn't had much chance to talk about what had passed between them that night.

"That's true," Eve said, not breaking eye contact. "How about you? You've given away the crutches, I see."

"Yeah, the leg's not too bad," Shelby replied. She pulled up the leg of her sweatpants to show the bandage wrapped around her calf. "Starting to itch like a son of a bitch, so I guess that's a good sign."

"What about your head?"

Shelby smiled. "Inside or out?"

Eve met the smile with one of her own and shrugged. "Either, or both," she said.

"The headaches stopped last week, which was a relief," Shelby said. That had been the most worrying of her injuries and she had been fearful that she would need to go see the doctors again, but the migraine-like pains had eased. "And otherwise, well, I guess I'm doing okay."

"Sleeping?"

Shelby nodded. "Better. Still a lot of nightmares, though." She leaned down and blew a raspberry on Pip's belly, a move that drew a chuckle from Eve. "What? He's just a big baby, so..."

"I'm not judging, really." Eve laughed. "As for the nightmares, you've got a lot to process. Don't fight them, they're doing a job. And you know you can always talk to me about them if they get troublesome again."

"I know, thanks."

They smiled at each other, unspoken emotions close to the surface for them.

"Well," Eve eventually said. "I've got some reports to write." She pushed herself upright and offered Shelby a hand to get up from the floor.

"Right, yes," Shelby said, noticing that even once she was on her feet, Eve continued to hold her hand, her thumb gently stroking the back of hers. "And...um...I'm willing to bet I don't have a scrap of food in the house, so I'm going to go and do some grocery shopping." The sensation was soft and warm and...incredibly distracting, she thought, realizing that neither of them had said anything for long seconds. "Right, yes."

Reluctantly they released hands.

"I'll see you later," Eve said as she retreated back up the stairs. "Have fun."

"You too," Shelby replied as she watched Eve close the door behind her. "Well...that went well."

EVE CLOSED THE door and leaned back against it, breathing out slowly. She knew that seeing Shelby again was going to be interesting after their late-night encounter, but she wasn't ready for the butterflies that took up residence in her stomach the moment she saw Shelby's car pull in to the driveway.

Relax, Eve, for god's sake. She pushed herself off the door and made her way to her study, trying to turn her thoughts to the report she had to write. But part of her wanted to turn around, go back and find Shelby, pin her to the nearest wall and kiss her senseless. *It's too soon, it's too soon, it's too soon. Keep thinking that.*

She sat down at the desk and pulled the pile of notes toward her. *Think about something else. Borderline personality disorder. That's always a buzz-kill. Yes, that's it. Run through the DSM-IV definitions or something.*

It didn't work for long, however. Eve groaned as she soon realized she was remembering the feel of Shelby's lips on her neck instead of writing up an assessment of the latest defendant Richard wanted her to analyze.

It's too soon, it's too soon, it's too soon.

SHELBY DROPPED THE paper-wrapped slices of shaved ham into the plastic container and tucked it into the last remaining free space in the picnic hamper she had bought yesterday. It was a Sunday morning three weeks after her return home. The sun was shining and she had a mind to get outdoors in the warmth. Ever since the night of the accident she had felt trapped indoors, either by her injuries, or by the need to concentrate on all the post-funeral chores. She felt like she hadn't seen the sun in weeks. And she had no intention of going on her own.

"Okay. Wine cooler, glasses, cutlery, plates...check. Ham, cheeses, crackers, sliced tomatoes, salt, pepper. Check. Potato salad, coleslaw, strawberries, cream. Check." All she was missing was..."Blanket." She walked down the hall to the linen cupboard and pulled out the thin blue and green plaid blanket that would make the perfect tablecloth.

On her way back to pack the blanket in the picnic basket, she passed the intercom up to Eve's floor.

Now or never, Shel.

She picked up handset and pressed the button. There were three phones upstairs and wherever Eve was she would hear it, Shelby knew. It didn't take long.

"Good morning. You're up early," Eve said.

"Well, I'm on a mission," Shelby replied. "Do you have anything to do today?"

"Nothing pressing. Why? What kind of mission?"

Shelby took a deep breath. "How do you feel about a long drive up in to the mountains and a picnic lunch, followed by a leisurely return through the wineries?"

There was a pause, and for a sinking moment she thought Eve was going to refuse. "Wow. That's quite a day, Ms. Macrossan." It was clear Eve was smiling, just from her tone and Shelby released her breath. "I would love to. When are we leaving?"

Shelby grinned. "Whenever you're ready. The picnic is packed."

"Want to take the convertible?"

Vroom, vroom, Shelby thought. "Can I drive?"

Eve laughed. "Don't push your luck, kid. See you in a few."

IN THE END Eve tossed Shelby the keys to the BMW and grinned at the look of delight on her face. "Have at it. Just don't scare me, okay? I'm in the mood for a relaxing day."

"Your wish is my command," Shelby said with a slight bow. She put the picnic basket on the back seat as Eve climbed into the passenger side. With a little skip in her step she moved around to the driver's side and slid in to the low-slung sports car. "Excellent," she purred as the engine thrummed into life. "Let's go."

Their route took them up a mountain road that curved and

snaked through thick, green forest before breaking into sunshine after about an hour. The two women spent the drive swapping music choices on the car's stereo system, laughing and talking about all manner of topics from current events to their respective jobs.

"Do you have a deadline for heading back to work?" Eve asked over the wind noise.

"Well, there's a show bumping in next week, but it's a touring company so I'm just assisting. It will be good to ease in to that," she said.

Eve nodded her agreement, watching as Shelby eased the powerful car around another tight hairpin. Smooth as silk, she observed. Sexy as hell, what's more. The thought caught her by surprise and she quickly refocused on the conversation.

"When is the next theatre company show?" she asked.

"Rehearsals start in three weeks," Shelby said. "But there are meetings with the set and lighting designers from next Wednesday."

"What's the show?"

"Would you believe, *How to Succeed in Business Without Really Trying*," Shelby said. "Sets by the million, and they want to put the show band behind the actors, from what I'm hearing."

"And that would be a bad thing?"

Shelby made an ambivalent gesture with her left hand. "Not necessarily. Fiddly as hell. A pain in the butt for the sound guys. And a waste of a perfectly good orchestra pit. But, hey. Mine is not to reason why."

"You just have to make it work," Eve said, smiling.

"Exactly."

There was silence, but for the wind noise and the music for a few more curves in the road.

"God, I love this car," Shelby said dreamily. "So smooth."

"Love me, love my car," Eve said without thinking and then held her breath as she realized what she'd said.

"No argument from me," Shelby answered calmly, and took another sharp turn.

THEY FOUND THE perfect spot on a slope of cleared land at the very pinnacle of the mountain. At the top of the grassed slope was a large Moreton Bay fig tree, its enormous and no doubt ancient canopy providing a shady spot with just enough dappled sunlight streaming through to keep them warm and comfortable. Eve spread the blanket out as Shelby carried the picnic basket from the car.

"Great view," she said, placing the basket down on a corner of the blanket and standing with her hands on her hips as she gazed out over the vista.

"Beautiful," Eve said.

They were facing east toward the ocean and beneath them was the long, green valley they had climbed, a patchwork of farming land, forests and the river, meandering down to the city and beyond it, the sea.

"If you had all the money in the world, where would you build your dream home?" Shelby asked as she sat down, cross-legged, on the blanket and reached for the basket. "Mountain or beach?"

Eve leaned back on her elbows, her legs crossed at the ankles. "This would do, right here," she said. "I'm not a beach person at all. Don't like them."

Shelby laughed. "How can you not like beaches? What's not too like?"

"Sand," said Eve. "Hate the stuff. Gets everywhere and serves no good purpose other than to separate the ocean from the people. What about you?"

"Beach," Shelby said without hesitation. "There's just something about the sound of the ocean that drops my blood pressure by about twenty points."

"See, that would just drive me crazy," Eve said. "Too much repetition." She looked at the spread that Shelby was laying out on the blanket. "Wow, Shelby, this looks fantastic. You've gone all out."

There was a pause as Shelby uncorked the cold bottle of white wine and poured two glasses, one of which she handed to Eve.

"I wanted it to be a special day," she said, smiling at Eve.

"I'm getting that impression," Eve said, taking the glass. "Cheers."

"Cheers," Shelby responded, clicking her glass against Eve's. "Here's to..." She thought about it. "Hmm...new beginnings?"

Eve nodded. "Good choice. New beginnings."

For the next hour they ate and chatted and lounged about, enjoying each other's company, the food and the wine. By the time they were done with all but dessert, both women were sitting shoulder to shoulder with their backs against the trunk of the mighty tree.

"Can I talk to you about something?" Shelby said after a significant, but comfortable silence.

"Silly question. Tell me."

"I never realized what you meant when you said that

everything was very fuzzy for you after Joe died."

Eve closed her eyes, remembering more than she really wanted to about that awful time in her life. "And now you do?"

"I think so, yes." Shelby glanced at the woman leaning against her left shoulder. "Is it still okay to talk about it? I don't want to dig stuff up if you don't want to go there."

Eve shook her head and smiled. "No, it's okay. It helps me too, you know."

"Okay, good." Shelby took a sip of her wine and drew her knees up, resting her forearms on them as she gazed out across the valley. "I feel like my head's been filled with cotton wool for weeks," she said.

"That's a good description of it."

"Not surprising. It's exactly the way you said it to me," Shelby said.

"Really? I don't remember that at all."

"Well, your head was full of cotton wool," Shelby reminded her. "It's like everything's been...muffled," she went on.

Eve looked at her, noting the serene expression on Shelby's face with interest. "And now?"

"Heaps better. I feel like I can actually organize things and have sensible conversations and remember them the next day, and not feel like I'm wading through molasses all the time."

Eve smiled. Progress. "That's great. How are you feeling about the coronial inquiry?"

Shelby sighed.

In any case involving an accident causing death, the state government, as a matter of routine, ordered an inquiry. Because the driver of the semi-trailer died in the accident, and because it happened late at night and no witnesses had come forward who actually saw it as it happened, this inquiry had relied mainly on police forensic work. Basically, the evidence showed that for some reason, the driver of the truck had ignored crossing signals and not realized until the last seconds that he was going to collide with the train. He'd tried to turn away but had ploughed into the side of the carriage in which Pauline and Ned Macrossan were berthed.

Shelby gave a statement but had not taken part in the hearing itself, much to her relief. The last thing she wanted to do was spend time looking at photographs and hearing testimony from other passengers and rescue workers. She had enough pictures in her head.

In the end the coroner ruled that the accident was due to driver negligence, probably brought about by fatigue, but that the primitive nature of the crossing signals had contributed to the crash.

"I was angry for a while," Shelby admitted. "But it's hard to stay angry with a dead man. Did you see his widow on the news?" Shelby shook her head in disbelief at the way the poor woman had been treated. "Nobody deserves to be screamed at for a mistake her husband made."

"No they don't." Eve took a mouthful of wine and swallowed. "Are you angry with your parents?"

There was a pause as Shelby thought about that. "What for? Going on the trip? No. They were just doing what they always did—turning an opportunity into a chance for some fun. Can't blame them for that. They didn't make it go pear-shaped."

Eve gazed off into the distance again. "What about for leaving you alone?" she asked quietly, knowing that was a question she hoped Shelby didn't ask her. She felt Shelby's eyes on her and rested her head back against the tree trunk.

"No, I don't think so," Shelby answered carefully. "You taught me a long time ago how to live separately from them." She saw the tiny smile at the corner of Eve's mouth at that comment. "Don't fob that off. You know damn well my biggest problem with them was always the boundaries. Without your help I suspect I'd be feeling a lot worse now than I do."

"You did the hard work," Eve said. "Perhaps that's a difference between grieving for parents and grieving for a partner," she wondered aloud.

Shelby leaned in and kissed Eve on the temple. "If he'd had a choice he would never have left you alone," she said softly.

Eve let the words soothe what was a very sore spot, still. She rested her head against Shelby's. "Oh, I know," she whispered. "But thank you."

She decided to turn the conversation back to Shelby. Part of her was very keen to know exactly where her head was at. "How are the nightmares?" she asked.

Shelby sighed. "A couple of times a week they wake me up," she said honestly. "Do you think I've got post-traumatic stress disorder?" Eve raised an eyebrow at that. "I've been Googling," Shelby said with a grin. "You knew I would." She laughed.

"A little knowledge is a dangerous thing, Shelby," Eve said with mock gravity. "But to answer your question, yes, I think you probably do. It would be amazing if you didn't, given what you went through and what you saw." She tilted her head and looked at Shelby. "Have you had any flashbacks?"

Shelby thought about it. "Not that I know of. Then again I haven't gotten on any trains either."

"Mmm, don't go buying trouble," Eve said. "When you have

to get on one, we'll deal with that together. Okay?"

"Okay. Thanks."

"No worries."

"Can we talk about something else, now, Doctor?" Shelby grinned at Eve, who laughed and drained her glass. Shelby took it and placed it, along with her own empty one, down on the blanket.

Something about Shelby's demeanor made Eve turn half toward her, anticipating that she had something else on her mind. *I can guess what that might be, if the twinkle in her eye is anything to go by.* "What's on your mind?" she asked.

"This," Shelby replied. She reached up and took Eve's face in her hands. Slowly she leaned in.

When Shelby's lips touched her's, Eve sank into the sensation, not pressing, just drifting, letting whatever happened, happen. It was delicious, prolonged, a precious moment in time.

She let the feelings wash over her. Shelby was gentle and tender, and the sensuality of it was almost overwhelming. Eve slid her hands around Shelby's waist, pulling her close, naturally deepening the kiss as she did so. She felt the tip of Shelby's tongue brush her own and she responded, feeling the passion accelerate between them.

Shelby groaned against her mouth. This was everything Eve imagined it could be. She felt Shelby pull away slightly, burying her face against Eve's neck, nuzzling and kissing the soft skin she found there.

Eve let her head tilt back, giving her more access, loving every touch and tingle. "God, Shelby," she gasped.

"Mmmmm?"

"It's been a very long time since someone made me literally breathless. You just did it in about thirty seconds."

In one quick movement Shelby lifted her head and kissed Eve again, but this time it was deep and open and filled with every ounce of passion she could muster. It was Eve who moaned this time, somewhat taken aback by her body's response, a hot wave of lust that washed through her. She recovered quickly, pushing up against Shelby, one hand sweeping through the soft auburn hair until she cupped the back of Shelby's head, her other hand sliding under Shelby's shirt, desperate to touch her, skin to skin.

"I want to get horizontal, right now," Eve said when their kiss broke. "I need to feel you."

Shelby didn't argue. Gently she pushed Eve on to her back on the blanket and stretched out along her right side, looking down at the blue eyes gazing up at her. She traced Eve's lips with the tip of her finger, watching as those eyes closed against the sensation, and then opened again.

"You have no idea how long I've been wanting to kiss you," Shelby said softly.

Eve smiled. "Actually I think I have the exact date written down in your file somewhere," she teased, brushing a lock of hair out of Shelby's face.

"Oh shut up," Shelby retorted. "That was different."

"I should hope so," Eve whispered, pulling Shelby down to her again. She controlled the kiss, teasing, sweeping her tongue across Shelby's, wanting to show her just how different it was.

Eve couldn't think in complete sentences anymore. Her universe narrowed down to the pocket of air she and Shelby lay in, and the sparks they were generating. She felt Shelby's hand slide to the buttons of her shirt and, one by one, she undid them, moving slowly down until she could push the shirt back to reveal Eve's bra. Shelby broke off the kiss long enough to look down and then she smiled.

"I knew it."

"Mmm, what did you know?" Eve murmured, aware that a deep blush was coloring her exposed skin.

"That beneath that buttoned-up," Eve bent down and kissed Eve's throat, "cool," and then the hollow at the base of her neck, "unflustered," along her collarbone, "elegant," slowly down her breastbone, "exterior, there was a sensual woman wearing sexy lingerie." She dropped a line of kisses along the edge of Eve's bra, tracing the soft, silky skin cupped by lace.

Eve could barely breathe and she felt herself arching up against Shelby's mouth. She was also exquisitely aware that they were out in the open. She felt more exposed than she had in a long, long time.

"Shelby...darling..."

"Mmmmm?"

"Take me home."

Shelby's head lifted and she met Eve's eyes, which were somehow a deeper shade of blue than they'd been just minutes ago. "Are you okay?" she asked, clearly scared that she had pushed too far, too fast.

"Shh, I'm perfect, sweetheart," Eve reassured. "I just have an urgent need to get you somewhere more private...and more comfortable...than this blanket. Take me home, please."

Shelby smiled broadly.

"I can do that."

SURPRISINGLY THE DRIVE home had not been as leisurely as the one they had taken up into the mountains. They hadn't said much, content to hold hands when Shelby didn't need both to negotiate the tight curves.

Shelby felt light-headed, almost disbelieving that what she had dreamed about for so long actually seemed to be happening, albeit differently from what she had imagined. It's all about timing, she realized. Wow.

EVE CONTENTED HERSELF with leaning back against the head-rest, the strong, warm hand in hers keeping her connected with a new reality. There should be a million questions I'm asking myself, she thought. Is this the right time? Is this right, period? But she felt none of the anxiety she'd half-expected around those issues. That alone told her that they had made the right choices. Professionally she felt she had satisfied every ethical consideration. With a wide safety margin, she reminded herself.

She closed her eyes and let the wind blow her hair, feeling safe in Shelby's hands.

Shelby's hands. Mmm.

"Eve?"

Shelby's voice pulled her from her reverie and she turned her face her, smiling back. "Yes?"

"You had the most interesting look on your face just then," Shelby said. "What was going on in your head?"

For her answer Eve lifted Shelby's hand to her lips and gently sucked the tip of her forefinger. Shelby nearly drove them off the road, the jolt was so strong.

Eve laughed as Shelby corrected quickly. "Easy there, tiger."

"Oh, woman," Shelby gasped. "You are wicked."

"This surprises you?" Eve teased, knowing very well that it surprised Shelby, who'd had no reason to suspect this facet of her personality even existed.

"Oh, I'm going to have to keep an eye on you, aren't I?" Shelby teased back, delighted to discover the playful side of her companion.

"I certainly hope so," Eve said, doing it again for good measure. This time Shelby managed to stay in the correct lane, though it took a fair amount of effort.

AN HOUR AND a half later they were walking into Eve's living room.

"Let me get the air-conditioning going," Eve said, making her way to the control panel on the wall in the kitchen.

"I'm just going to...um...dump this stuff downstairs," Shelby replied, indicating the picnic basket and blanket. For a moment she stood uncertainly, suddenly unsure if she was assuming too much in thinking she should come straight back up.

"Do me a favor?" Eve called back over her shoulder. "Bring that Kitaro CD when you come back up?"

Well, that answered that question, Shelby thought, grinning as she turned on her heel and headed down to her apartment. "Sure."

UNAWARE OF THE momentary lapse in self-confidence going on behind her, Eve adjusted the ducted A/C system, trying to cool the house down in a hurry. It had been cool up on the mountain but apparently had been another humid stinker down here in the city.

She busied herself finding clean glasses and pulling another bottle of wine from the bottom shelf of the refrigerator. Truthfully, she was having an attack of nerves. She knew very well where the evening ahead was going.

Well, I don't know, she admitted. I can imagine. It's not like I've ever... It was the first time she'd ever really acknowledged to herself that she was about to wander into what was, for her, virgin territory. So to speak. And with a woman who has plenty of experience, what's more. She wondered if that had even occurred to Shelby yet. I guess we're about to find out. She breathed deeply and tried to calm the butterflies in her stomach.

Shelby came back in carrying the CD and walked over to the stereo system. She slid the disk in and waited for it to begin, adjusting the volume as the first strains of the music drifted out.

"Thanks for lending me this, by the way," Shelby said. "Awesome music."

"It's my pleasure." Eve handed Shelby her glass of wine. "And if it helps you sleep, all the better." She took Shelby's hand and pulled her over to the couch. They sat down next to each other and Eve took the opportunity to snuggle in against Shelby's side, pulling her arm around her shoulders.

"Mmm nice," Shelby said.

"The wine?"

"That too. Eve?"

"Mmm?"

"You okay?"

Eve looked up into wide brown eyes that held more than a

little concern and uncertainty.

"Very much so," she replied. "Are you?"

Shelby nodded. "I'm pretty sure I'm a lot more than okay," she said. "I guess I'm just wary of us rushing."

Eve sat up and took Shelby's wine glass, placing them both on the coffee table in front of them. She turned back to Shelby and cupped her chin with gentle fingers.

"Honey." She waited for Shelby to make eye contact. "How long have we known each other?"

"Um...But you were off-limits for a lot of that and now..."

Eve nodded, knowing that, truthfully, they had made a giant change in the last twenty-four hours even if it had been a long...long...long time coming.

"Shelby I want to kiss you and touch you and continue on from where we left off up on that mountain. I want to so badly my fingertips—among other things—are tingling right now, just thinking about it." Shelby grinned and Eve laughed. "And don't you just love that, Miss Ego."

"Oh, like you're not having exactly the same effect on me."

A flash of shyness mixed with pleasure swept through Eve. "Really?"

Shelby's eyes widened. "You doubt that? I must be losing my touch. Eve, you had me...incredibly...unbelievably..."

"Turned on?" There was a hopeful look on Eve's face that made Shelby smile. But it also made her think.

"Yes, turned on." A light dawned. "Wait a minute." Shelby took Eve's hands and looked at her intently. "You've never done this before, have you?" she asked gently.

"Well, obviously, I've done similar things before."

"With a woman?"

"No, not with a woman," she confessed, feeling the blush rise on her cheeks.

Eve watched Shelby's eyes widen. "Not even...?"

Eve shook her head. "Not even the *de rigueur* high school kissing crush, or the standard college experimentation, no," she said. She shrugged. "What can I tell you? It was a very sheltered life. And then I met Joe."

Shelby blinked rapidly, processing the privileged position she found herself in. Finally, she grinned. "You're going to enjoy this," she said, now sporting her own blush.

"Oh, I hope so," Eve said softly, sliding her hands up Shelby's arms and leaning in for a deep, soft kiss that left them both breathless.

"I have a suggestion," Shelby said, somewhat hoarsely. Eve was pushing her down on to her back along the soft leather of the couch, kissing her neck and collarbone as they tangled their legs around each other.

"Mmmm, what's that?" Eve gasped as she felt Shelby's long thigh slide between her legs and press up against her heat. She matched the movement, eliciting a groan from Shelby.

Shelby tried hard to slow her movements. "I think," she whispered in Eve's ear, nibbling between words. "I think we should just enjoy what we're doing right now for as long as we want and when you're ready, we can go further." she said. "Doesn't have to be tonight." She groaned again as Eve's hands pressed against the small of her back, increasing the contact between them. "Though if you keep doing that I may not be responsible for my own actions."

A throaty chuckle greeted that suggestion and for several more minutes they explored and caressed and enjoyed every second of their interaction.

Eve pulled back from the kiss and held Shelby's gaze. "Thank you," she whispered. "For understanding."

"Shh." Shelby brushed a finger over Eve's lips. "I want this to be perfect for you. I want it to be exactly what you want."

"And what about what you want?" Eve asked.

"Already got it," Shelby said, nuzzling the soft cleavage that was too temptingly close to resist.

Eve groaned. "You're going to kill me." The muffled laugh from the woman beneath her was unexpected, but highly pleasurable. "Come up here and kiss me," she murmured.

"Your wish is my command," Shelby burred.

HOURS LATER SHELBY lay in bed, her hands behind her head as she gazed at the ceiling. The two women had parted around midnight, flustered and well and truly hot and bothered. They had agreed to temper their pace, and given Eve had to be up just after dawn and Shelby would be back at work for the first time since the train crash, they'd both decided that abstention was the most sensible decision.

Stupid sensible, Shelby thought. It's not like I can sleep anyway. Her skin felt flushed despite the cold shower she had just before pulling on an old t-shirt and climbing into bed.

She went over the events of the day, a process that only resulted in raising her temperature even further. She even contemplated taking matters into her own hands but then decided that there was a certain appeal in waiting. Anticipation, she decided, can be a fine, fine thing.

She rolled on to her left side and tried closing her eyes for another attempt at sleep. A sound from her living room made her ears prick up momentarily, but as she had left the door to Eve's part of the house open, she figured Pip was wandering in to take up his usual spot at the foot of her bed.

Sure enough, soft footsteps picked their way across her carpet and when the mattress behind her moved under quickly applied weight, Shelby reacted.

"Piiiip. Get off the bed. You know better, boy."

"Nothing 'boy' about it," came the whisper, warm breath brushing against her ear. "Woof woof."

Shelby turned into Eve's embrace, her arms suddenly full of warm, delightfully naked woman. Even in the dark their mouths found each other with a sureness that took her breath away and drew moans from both of them.

"You have too many clothes on," Eve said when they drew breath.

"Not for long," Shelby replied and with one quick motion she pulled the t-shirt up and off, throwing it into a distant corner of the room.

Their bodies were in full contact now for the first time, breast on breast, belly to belly, thighs pressed to hot, wet centers. For minutes they rolled, tangled, arched and cupped each other, wordless and in sync. Then Eve couldn't bear the pressure any longer.

"Shelby," she gasped.

"Yes." Breathing each other's air.

"Make love to me. Now. Please, right now." Shelby groaned, deep and heartfelt. "And then teach me how to make love to you."

"You already are," Shelby whispered back, rolling Eve on to her back and arching in to her. "You don't need lessons."

Another kiss silenced her momentarily. "Now, darling. Now."

Chapter Fourteen

Today and tomorrow

I'M TURNING FORTY. The thought amazed Shelby. Forty. That's like...old.

Eve had thrown her a party. Most of Shelby's friends and colleagues, and quite a few of Eve's as well, gathered at the house for what turned out to be a very pleasant evening full of music and laughter.

She and Eve had been a couple for just shy of eighteen months and had settled into a comfortable relationship which had enriched both their lives. They hadn't been secretive about it, preferring to be open and out, even with Eve's older friends who had known her since the early years of her marriage.

It had cost her some of those friends, Shelby knew, although Eve rarely bothered to speak of it. "If they can't deal with it, then I don't need those kinds of friends," she'd said after one particularly nasty encounter with one ex-school chum.

It bothered Shelby, though. She didn't like the idea it cost Eve to be with her, however much she wanted to believe it didn't matter.

But that was something they'd come to terms with over the months as they found their footing as a couple. They still maintained their separate living spaces in the house, but it was a rare night when they didn't share a bed.

Work was much as it had been for the last few years. Shelby had been content with that, needing the stability and safety of knowing her role in life after the death of her parents. She had to admit, though, that there were times when she felt restless and bored with dealing with the same personalities and challenges.

But overall, she was happy. She put the occasional stirrings of discontent down to turning forty. I'm turning forty, she thought again, shaking her head. Unbelievable.

Shelby sat on the verandah, overlooking the canal at the back of Eve's house, watching the moonlight on the water as she sipped on a cold beer. The last of the guests had just left and she was waiting for Eve to come back and join her. It was a fun evening, but now she wanted some quality time with her partner, alone.

She felt rather than heard Eve's approach and when arms wrapped around her neck from behind and a familiar chin dropped on to her shoulder, she raised her hands and clasped Eve's forearms.

"Hello, darling," Eve said softly in her ear.

"Hi, gorgeous," she replied.

"You are so old."

"Hahahahaha. Thank you so much." Shelby laughed, mock slapping the warm arm under her hand. "So kind."

Eve laughed as well and moved around to sit down in the canvas chair next to Shelby's. "Well, be content with the thought that no matter how old you are, sweetheart, I'll always be fifteen years older."

"True, true," Shelby said, taking another swig of beer.

"Did you have a good time?"

Shelby looked at her contentedly. "I had a great time," she said. "Thank you so much for my party. It was an awesome present."

"Oh, that wasn't your present," Eve said, taking the beer from Shelby's hand and swallowing down a mouthful.

"It wasn't?" Shelby replied, honestly surprised.

"No. Your real present is on the chair next to the bath in my en suite."

"All right, let's go," Shelby said, jumping out of her chair with excitement.

"Well, hang on now," Eve said hastily, grabbing Shelby's hand and holding her back. "There's just one rule."

"And what's that?"

"You have to take a bath with me before you can open it," Eve said, smiling up at her.

"Oh, I think I can manage that," Shelby said before she leaned down and kissed Eve softly. "Come on."

Ten minutes later they were lounging in steaming water, gentle jets caressing them with bubbles. Eve had filled the bathroom with candles, sprinkled the surface of the water with rose petals and added essential oils. Shelby was in heaven. She lay back against Eve's chest, eyes closed, humming softly to the music playing quietly in the background.

"You are just perfect," she murmured, rubbing her hands slowly along Eve's thighs, which were wrapped around her.

Eve chuckled. "You're such a sucker for romance," she replied, sliding her hands around Shelby's waist and pulling her closer.

"No question," Shelby said. "This day can't get any better, darling. You can take that present back. I don't need it. Everything's perfect."

"Oh, I don't think you want me to do that," Eve said. She

lifted her right hand out of the water, dried it on the towel she had draped on the side of the bath and picked up the envelope from the nearby chair. "Open it."

"Okay, you twisted my arm." Shelby dried her hands as well and took the envelope. "Is it going to fall out all over the place?" She sat up and turned to face Eve.

"Not if you're careful."

Shelby slid her thumb along the seal and cracked it open. Inside was a typed letter on official letterhead. She pulled it out and dropped the empty envelope over the side so she could unfold the paper. She read it, her eyes widening as she took in the words.

"Flights to London?" Oh my god. "Business class flights to London? Seriously?"

Eve grinned at the childlike expression of happiness on Shelby's face. She had been to London several times, but to theatre-mad Shelby, the city was a dream destination she was yet to get to.

"Seriously," she said. "Plus there's accommodation booked in the centre of the West End. Nothing too flashy, but we'll be comfortable and close to all the action."

Shelby gazed at her like she had turned to gold and grown angel's wings. "Have I told you lately how much I love you?" she said. "This is so...generous...Eve...are you sure?" She was dumbfounded.

"Darling, come here." Eve took the letter from Shelby and placed it back on the chair, before reaching for her and pulling her closer. "You only turn forty once, youngster, and I love you. Besides I want to come with you and show you one of my favorite cities."

Shelby kissed her soundly. "I adore you. Thank you."

"It's entirely my pleasure. And I adore you too, by the way."

"Of course you do. I'm entirely adorable." Shelby kissed her again, this time more slowly and with much more intent.

"But so old."

EVE HAD TO laugh. Shelby had leapt off the double-decker bus like a puppy chasing a butterfly, dodging people on the pavement, then standing and staring up Shaftesbury Avenue, as the flow of pedestrians moved around her.

They had been in London barely a day and even though the weather was foul—cold and raining—Shelby had been barely containable when they woke in their hotel room this morning.

Eve joined her on the pavement and stood shoulder to

shoulder with her, looking up the famous street and wondering if she was seeing it quite the way Shelby was. To her it looked crowded, wet, and not a little grimy, but Shelby clearly had stars in her eyes.

"Look at it, Eve," Shelby said excitedly. She lifted her arm and pointed out the theatres that dotted the landscape of Shaftesbury Avenue. "Six of the most famous theatres in the world. On one street." She laughed out loud. "The Apollo—1901—*Jerusalem's* playing there." She swung around and pointed in the direction of another. "The Shaftesbury—1911—*Hairspray's* been playing there since the end of 2007. The Lyric—1888, for crying out loud—*Thriller's* on there. The Gielgud—1906—*Avenue Q* is on. But not for much longer," she said hastily. "The Broadway production of *Hair*'s transferring there soon. The Palace—1891—*Priscilla, Queen of the Desert's* playing there. And the Queen's—1907—the revival of *Les Miserables* has been playing there since God was a boy."

Eve laughed with delight. "Shelby, how on earth do you keep all that in your head? Did you swallow the theatre listings or something?" She hooked her arm through Shelby's as they walked north up Shaftesbury Avenue, leaving Piccadilly Circus behind them.

"Well, how do you remember all that stuff about narcissistic personality disorder and cognitive dissonance and all that?" Shelby replied. "It's my thing. Eve, this place is...Mecca...for stage managers."

Eve had never thought about it like that. "Wow. I don't think psychologists have a Mecca," she said. "Unless you count that museum that claims to have a box of Sigmund Freud's cigars." She grinned and squeezed Shelby's arm. "So what do you want to see?"

"It would be easier to decide what I don't want to see," Shelby replied.

"Oh my."

IN THE END there had indeed been few shows they didn't see in the four weeks they were in London. They also packed in a lot of sightseeing, but the principle delight for Eve was watching Shelby's passion for the history and culture of London's theatre districts. It had been a long time since she'd seen Shelby so fired up and absorbed. She also noticed the slightly wistful expression on Shelby's face on many nights as they sat in their seats, waiting for the house lights to dim and the performances to begin.

And it had Eve thinking.

It was their last night in the city and she and Shelby had decided to treat themselves to a luxurious meal at the restaurant of one of the more globally recognized celebrity chefs about town. The food had been superb and as they waited for their coffee and liqueurs their conversation had lulled into a companionable silence. Eve decided this was the moment for the discussion she'd been contemplating for much of their London holiday.

"Can I ask you something?" she said, after the waiter put her latte and glass of Cognac in front of her.

Shelby raised an eyebrow. It wasn't usual for Eve to feel the need to qualify a conversation that way. "Of course. What's up?"

Eve reached for her hand and held it on the tabletop. "Nothing dire," she replied, smiling in reassurance. "Just something I've been thinking about and I wanted to get your thoughts."

"Okay, fire away." Shelby took a sip of her brandy, watching Eve over the top of the glass.

"Why aren't you working here in London?" Eve asked, cutting right to the chase.

Shelby laughed in surprise. "For about a million reasons," she said. "Why?"

"Tell me some of the reasons."

Shelby tilted her head, somewhat baffled about the question and why it was being asked.

"You mean apart from the fact that I have a perfectly good job back home, that I have a life that I love, a partner I adore and no reason at all to want or need more than those things?"

Eve nodded, deciding to get past the slightly defensive tone to Shelby's answer. "Yes, apart from those things. Take those things as given."

There was a pause as Shelby considered a more serious answer to what was obviously a question that Eve had been thinking about a lot.

"Well, let's see," she said. "For a start, it's London. The best of the best. Everybody wants to work here. There are this many theatres ..." she held the tips of her thumb and forefinger close together, "... and about a billion stage managers who want to work in them. The math alone is insane."

"Okay. Put that aside for a moment as well," Eve said. "What else is bad about the idea?"

"You don't just decide to work 'in London'," Shelby went on. "You work for one of several production companies—like Really Useful, or Ambassador—and for the most part those companies have theatres all over the country, in regional centers and the other big cities. Working a show in London comes after working endless out of town shows and theatres."

Eve nodded. "Don't a few of those companies also have theatres in New York?" she asked.

"Yes," Shelby replied, impressed that Eve had obviously done some research on the subject. "Ambassador runs productions on Broadway. And in Sydney and Melbourne, actually."

"So, a job with one of those companies might also give you the chance to work in New York?"

Shelby was really puzzled. "Eve, where are you going with this?"

"I just think it might be interesting to consider the possibilities," she said, shrugging slightly.

"I'm happy," Shelby said. "Why try and fix what's not broken?"

"Because you might just end up with something even better," Eve said, tugging at Shelby's hand until she met her eyes. "Look, I'm not trying to stir up a whole hornet's nest here. But I've seen how excited this place makes you. And I like seeing that twinkle in your eye."

"I have a twinkle," Shelby said. "All the time." Eve swore she could detect a slight pout.

"Honey, it wasn't a criticism. Just think about it a little? For me?"

"What's the point?" Shelby said, pulling her hand out of Eve's and folding her arms, elbows resting on the table. "I'm a stage manager with a theatre company in a city that thinks cane-toad racing is the height of sophistication, in a country where the words 'cultural cringe' still get a regular run in the Arts pages. And it's all about as far away from London as you can get and still be an Earthling. Why would Cameron Macintosh even consider giving me a job?"

"Don't do that," Eve said quietly, disturbed that it hadn't taken much to bring out what was clearly a level of discontent in Shelby that she hadn't anticipated.

"Don't do what?" Shelby muttered, taking another mouthful of brandy.

"Don't talk down what you do and what you've achieved. Look, I didn't mean to make this into a big thing. I just wanted to give you another perspective to look at."

Shelby didn't meet her gaze. "I don't want to look at it," she said gruffly.

"Why not, sweetheart?" Eve asked, feeling she had to tease something out of Shelby for the first time in a very long time.

"Too scary." Finally, wide brown eyes looked at her and

their message was plain to Eve. Leave it be. Please.

"Okay, love," she said. But we're going to talk about this again. Sooner rather than later.

THE PHONE WAS ringing.

Shelby groaned. It's Sunday morning. Go away.

It kept ringing.

Eve will get it, she thought as she rolled over and buried her head under a pillow. Sure enough the phone stopped ringing and Shelby could just hear Eve's low tones talking to whoever had been rude enough to call before noon on Sunday.

Shelby and Eve had been home from their London vacation for about a month and had slipped back into their usual routine. Shelby was managing a show which had opened the week before and looked like having a decent run. Last night they had played to a packed house and the cast and crew had partied hard until dawn.

Shelby was a rare attendee at those parties lately, preferring to come home to Eve's warm, sleeping form in her bed. Last night she had partied, however, and she and Eve had spent a rare night apart.

That's okay, Shelby thought as she let her mind drift, hopefully back to sleep. She knew Eve would finish whatever chore or report she was working on and then come and crawl in with her for a catnap and maybe something a little more vigorous. She smiled into the pillow. Love is good.

Sure enough, a couple of minutes later, Eve padded into the bedroom, carrying the Sunday papers and a plate of buttered toast. She put the plate and papers on the bedside table, slipped off her dressing gown and slid in behind Shelby, wrapping her arms around her waist and pulling her into her lap.

"Good morning," she whispered in Shelby's right ear, placing a tiny kiss on its edge.

"Mmm, hello," Shelby burred, putting her hand on top of Eve's and wiggling back further into her lap. "Did you miss me?"

"Silly question. My feet got cold."

"Oh, hardy har har. And here I was thinking I was more to you than a hot water bottle."

"Only in summer, darling," Eve teased. To make up for it she kissed a slow trail from the nape of Shelby's neck out to the tip of her shoulder, an action that elicited a sound that could best be described as a purr from Shelby.

"Keep doing that and you may have to give me the full treatment, doctor," Shelby murmured.

"I can do that," Eve replied, moving a hand up and cupping

the soft breast it encountered.

AN HOUR LATER, Shelby drifted in and out of sleep happily as Eve read the paper.

"Who was on the phone?" Shelby muttered in one of her more lucid moments.

"Oh, it was for you, actually," Eve replied as she turned the page and refolded the broadsheet. "Gil. He said to call him back once you were up and about. It wasn't urgent."

Shelby rolled on to her back and stared at the ceiling. "That's weird," she said.

"What is?"

"He was at the party after the show. Why didn't he just talk to me about it then?"

Eve looked at her over the top of her reading glasses. "I don't know, love. But you'll find out when you call him. I'd leave it a while longer though. He sounded very tired and cranky."

Shelby sniggered. "I'm not surprised. He was tanked. Took one look at the box office receipts for the week and shouted the bar." She grinned. "Sounds like someone woke him up a little too early."

"Mhm. Want some toast?"

"GIL? IT'S SHELBY. How's the head?"

A loud groan was her answer. "Don't even talk about it," he replied. "What the hell was I drinking anyway?"

"Sambuca," Shelby said promptly. "Shots and shots and shots of the stuff."

"Jesus. Isn't it part of your job to stop me making an arse of myself?"

Shelby grinned. "I'd have to check the fine print on my contract, mate, but somehow I don't think so."

Gil grunted and she could hear him shifting the phone to his other ear. She was on the back verandah and she sat down in the swing chair as her boss sorted himself out.

"Speaking of your contract, Shel," he said. "You're being headhunted."

Shelby's head jerked up in surprise. "I'm what?"

"Headhunted. Look, I got a call this morning — very bloody early this morning, I can tell you — from an English bloke from Nimax," he said.

Holy shit, Shelby thought. "Nimax? As in Nimax Theatres

Limited? As in Nica Burns and Max Weitzenhoffer? As in the owners of the Lyric, the Apollo, the Duchess and the Garrick? In London?"

"Yeah, that would be the one. Jesus, what are you? Some kind of theatre Wikipedia or something? What a freak." He snorted with laughter.

Shelby wasn't laughing. Her stomach was doing loop-the-loops and threatening to come out her ears.

"What did...what was his name? What did he want?" she asked.

"Can't remember his name. Paul something. Bannerman, that's right. Paul Bannerman," Gil said. "Anyway, he's Nica Burns' right hand, apparently. They're looking to recruit some internationals. I gave him your name and resume."

Shelby felt like a fish out of water, gasping for air. "You did...you did what?"

"Jesus, Shel. What's up with you? You sound more hungover than I am," he grumbled. "They're coming out here in three weeks to interview candidates. I gave him your name. They want to talk to you."

Shelby switched her phone to the other ear in case she was having some kind of auditory malfunction. "Why on earth would you give them my name?"

"Because you're good, ya goose, why else? You're the best I've got and don't kid yourself. It would look really good if one of our own ended up with Nimax, in London. D'you think I'm an idiot?"

Shelby barely heard the rest of the conversation, registering that she needed to be in Sydney three weeks from Monday, portfolio in hand, for her interview. She said goodbye to Gil and hung up.

EVE FOUND HER there fifteen minutes later. Shelby was gazing out over the canal, deep in thought. Eve slid in next to her as the chair swung gently, pushed by Shelby's foot on the verandah railing.

"You okay?" Eve asked, concerned by the faraway look on her face.

"A bit stunned actually," Shelby replied, looking over her shoulder at Eve. Quickly she recounted the gist of the conversation with Gil.

"Wow. Shelby that's fantastic," Eve said, wrapping her arms around Shelby and squeezing.

"Is it?" Shelby answered. "I'm not that sure. What if they

offer me something?"

"What if they do?" Eve replied quickly. "What an opportunity!"

Shelby turned around and took Eve's hands, an intent look in her eyes. "Come with me," she said.

"To Sydney? Of course. We'll make a weekend of it, take in a show," Eve said, deliberately misinterpreting the question, knowing that this discussion could go anywhere.

"No, not Sydney. To London."

Eve smiled gently. "Honey, don't you think we should wait and see if they offer you something before we have that conversation?" *I need you to put some more thought into this, my love,* she thought.

But Shelby wasn't going to let it go so easily. "You're the one who wanted to have this conversation in London a month ago," she said. "Well, I want to have the conversation now."

Eve sighed. She had rehearsed this in her head so many times over the last few months, knowing that it was bound to happen. But now that it was here, the thought of the potential hurt for them both was daunting.

"Shelby," she said. "Over the years...when you were my client...we had several conversations about developmental stages. Remember?"

Exasperated, Shelby dropped Eve's hands and stood up in a hurry, stalking to the railing and looking out over the canal. "You're not really going to fall back on some psychobabble when it comes to us, are you?" she asked, her voice dangerously flat and angry. "This is us we're talking about here."

Eve nodded. "Yes it is. And it's relevant." She took in the defensive body language and the anger washing off Shelby's back. "Darling, please come and sit back down." No response. "Please."

It took a few seconds, but finally she saw Shelby's posture ease and she turned back around. She returned to Eve's side, sitting in the chair.

Eve took a deep breath. "Love, the age difference between us has never been an issue. But the fact is, I'm fifteen years older than you."

"Exactly. It's never been an issue. So why make it one now?"

Eve took her hand again. "Because things change. Two people in a relationship — they begin in different places, they come together and travel beside each other. Depending on what developmental stage each of them is in they travel together for a long time or things change, and paths diverge." She could see Shelby didn't want to hear any of this, but it had to be said.

"I'm fifty-five years old," she said. "My life has reached the point I've been aiming for most of my adulthood. My practice is established, I'm achieving the things I've always wanted to with my clients, working things my way. Financially I'm in a good place. I own my own home. I can live the rest of my life the way I always wanted to, securely and with a safety net. My relationships with friends are long-term and well-established.

"I'm where I want to be, Shelby. At the place I've been working toward."

Shelby looked so miserable Eve wished this conversation had never begun.

"And where do I fit into that?" Shelby asked quietly.

"I love you with all my heart," Eve replied, catching and holding eye contact with Shelby. "You know that, I know you do." She waited until Shelby nodded. "But, to me, that doesn't mean that I have the right to hold you in my life if it's not the right thing for you." She held a finger against Shelby's lips as she saw her start to object. "Wait, let me get this out.

"Shelby, you're forty. You have another quarter of a century—twenty-five whole years—to work and build your career and establish yourself. Do you really want to spend that quarter-century in exactly the same place you are now?" She watched the confusion on Shelby's face at this new perspective.

"This is where those fifteen years between us become so important, my love. We're in the same place right now. But for me this place is an end point, of sorts. For you, it's another step along the way." She paused, wanting to be sure Shelby understood her. "Does that make any sense?"

The lump in Shelby's throat prevented her from saying anything. She nodded, the movement causing the tears that welled in her eyes to spill over. Eve reached up and brushed a tear away with the pad of her thumb. Shelby closed her eyes against the tenderness of the gesture.

"I love you so much," Eve said, allowing the wistfulness she felt to sound in her voice. "But I couldn't bear it if I was the reason you stopped moving forward, stopped learning and growing. I'd rather let you go than do that to you."

Shelby leaned forward and rested her forehead on Eve's shoulder, her face buried in the softness of the silk shirt Eve was wearing. "Please stop talking now," she begged.

She knows I'm right, Eve realized as she felt Shelby's tears soak through the shirt. She wrapped her arms around Shelby's lanky frame and held her in the closest hug she could muster. Love is good.

THE TWO WOMEN at the departure gate drew attention to themselves simply by being so still and totally absorbed in each other. They stood, forehead to forehead, eyes closed, their arms around each other.

"You've got everything?" Eve asked quietly. "Passport, boarding pass, clean hanky?"

Shelby smiled at that last item. "Yes," she replied.

They lapsed back into silence. Everything they wanted to say to each other had been said many, many times since Shelby had accepted Nimax's offer of a job in England. All that was left was the love and the acceptance.

"This is the final boarding call for Qantas flight fifty-one to London via Singapore. Would all remaining passengers please make their way to Gate fifteen for immediate departure. Qantas flight fifty-one, now boarding at Gate fifteen."

The two women didn't move.

"That's me," Shelby whispered.

"I know."

They opened their eyes and got lost in each other one more time.

"Call me when you get there," Eve said. Shelby nodded.

"Rufus' pills are on top of my fridge," Shelby said.

"Shelby..."

"...and don't get them mixed up with Pip's heartworm tablets."

"Shelby..."

"...and..."

Warm lips silenced her. When they parted, both women had tears on their cheeks.

"Get on the plane. Please. Or this is going to become a spectacle," Eve said, trying to smile.

Shelby swallowed and began to back away. "Thank you," she whispered. "Thank you for everything."

"Shh," Eve couldn't bear this. "I love you, Shelby."

"I love you, Eve."

"You know where I am."

"I do."

"I'm always here."

One last look and Shelby turned on her heel and walked away.

SHELBY GLANCED AT the stopwatch. Seven minutes until curtain. As she had done with every show she'd ever managed, she walked out on to the stage to make her last check before giving the players their call.

This time is a little different, though. This was the West End, and her first show in charge in London. At the Garrick, no less. She still had to pinch herself on a regular basis. History oozed out of the wings. She could almost hear the ghosts of all the legends who had performed here. Six months of schlepping around the regional theatres in Brighton, Birmingham, Glasgow and Liverpool had led her here.

Shelby walked back to her desk in the wing, stage left and keyed the microphone to the green room backstage. "Ms. Walters, Mr. Stewart, this is your five-minute call. Five minutes, ladies and gentlemen."

She switched off the mike and touched the card that she had placed on top of the desk earlier in the day. It was the card Eve had sent her so long ago, the night she had come to see the show at the Arts Center back home. Back when we had barely begun, she thought. Shelby ran her finger over the familiar handwriting, smiling at the words.

"Thank you, Eve. For this," she murmured. She flicked the transmit button on her headset.

"House lights down. Standby curtain and light cues one and two." She waited, counting the beats. "And...curtain. Light cue one...go. Light cue two...go."

The actors kicked into the first scene and Shelby breathed again.

Thank you, Eve. For everything.

Other Cate Swannell titles published by
Yellow Rose Books

Heart's Passage

Jo Madison is a yacht skipper in the Whitsunday Islands of Australia's Great Barrier Reef. She has a dark and violent past she is trying to leave far behind her, and the last thing on her mind is love. But when Cadie Jones, long-time partner of a U.S. senator, sails in to her life, her priorities change.

There's no rest for the formerly wicked, however and Jo's past comes back to haunt her, throwing herself and Cadie into mortal danger. Jo is forced to rely on skills and weapons she had thought long-buried, while Cadie struggles to balance her Midwest life against her attraction to the mysterious woman.

Set in the splendor of Australia's tropics, *Heart's Passage* traces Jo and Cadie's rocky path to an uncertain future.

ISBN 978-1-932300-09-3

No Ocean Deep

No Ocean Deep continues the story of Jo and Cadie as they work to establish their relationship and their life together in the tropical islands of north Australia. Jo must reconcile with her parents, after 15 years spent leading a double life, before she can begin to forgive herself for her dark past. Meanwhile, Cadie has unfinished business with her former partner, the dangerous and volatile Naomi, whose political career and sanity are balanced on a knife edge. Jo and Cadie endure separation and an emotional rollercoaster that takes them from the Great Barrier Reef, to the wilds of the Australian outback, and to the suburbs of Chicago, Illinois and Madison, Wisconsin.

ISBN 978-1-932300-54-3

Other Yellow Rose Titles You Might Enjoy:

Casa Parisi
by Janet Albert

Lucia Parisi holds the world within her grasp until one tragic afternoon when everything slips through her fingers. In an attempt to re-build her shattered life she moves back home to the Finger Lakes region of central New York State where she opens a winery. On the surface the pieces of her new life are falling into place except for one vital thing...Lucia can't find a way to heal her heart.

French Canadian winemaker, Juliet Renard, is rapidly gaining a reputation as a rising young talent among local winery owners. She's paid her dues and now it is time to leave her current job as an assistant in the hopes of finding a position as a head winemaker.

When Lucia asks a friend if she knows any available winemakers, her friend encourages her to bring Juliet in for an interview. For both women, their meeting marks a major turning point, but for vastly different reasons. Lucia is forced to take a look at what tragedy has done to her and Juliet discovers something about herself that changes her life forever.

ISBN 978-1-61929-015-0

Callie's Dilemma
by Vicki Stevenson

While attending a convention for authors and fans of chick lit, Callie Delaney, closeted reigning queen of mainstream romance, meets Dale Kirby, irresistible fitness instructor for the health club at the hotel that's hosting the event. She also inadvertently walks into the prelude to a murder. Although Callie is unaware of the significance of what she sees, the killer is not, and he embarks on a relentless campaign to eliminate the only witness to his crime.

With help from Dale's LGBT family, the women set out to uncover the motivation for the threats against Callie, identify her mysterious stalker, and ultimately prove him guilty of murder. As a fragile relationship develops between Dale and Callie, they are forced to confront escalating danger and the irresolvable conflict between the demands of Callie's public image and the reality of her personal desire.

ISBN 978-1-61929-003-7

OTHER YELLOW ROSE PUBLICATIONS

Brenda Adcock	Soiled Dove	978-1-935053-35-4
Brenda Adcock	The Sea Hawk	978-1-935053-10-1
Brenda Adcock	The Other Mrs. Champion	978-1-935053-46-0
Janet Albert	Twenty-four Days	978-1-935053-16-3
Janet Albert	A Table for Two	978-1-935053-27-9
Janet Albert	Casa Parisi	978-1-61929-015-0
Georgia Beers	Thy Neighbor's Wife	1-932300-15-5
Georgia Beers	Turning the Page	978-1-932300-71-0
Carrie Brennan	Curve	978-1-932300-41-3
Carrie Carr	Destiny's Bridge	1-932300-11-2
Carrie Carr	Faith's Crossing	1-932300-12-0
Carrie Carr	Hope's Path	1-932300-40-6
Carrie Carr	Love's Journey	978-1-932300-65-9
Carrie Carr	Strength of the Heart	978-1-932300-81-9
Carrie Carr	The Way Things Should Be	978-1-932300-39-0
Carrie Carr	To Hold Forever	978-1-932300-21-5
Carrie Carr	Trust Our Tomorrows	978-1-61929-011-2
Carrie Carr	Piperton	978-1-935053-20-0
Carrie Carr	Something to Be Thankful For	1-932300-04-X
Carrie Carr	Diving Into the Turn	978-1-932300-54-3
Carrie Carr	Heart's Resolve	978-1-61929-051-8
Cronin and Foster	Blue Collar Lesbian Erotica	978-1-935053-01-9
Cronin and Foster	Women in Uniform	978-1-935053-31-6
Pat Cronin	Souls' Rescue	978-1-935053-30-9
Anna Furtado	The Heart's Desire	1-932300-32-5
Anna Furtado	The Heart's Strength	978-1-932300-93-2
Anna Furtado	The Heart's Longing	978-1-935053-26-2
Melissa Good	Eye of the Storm	1-932300-13-9
Melissa Good	Hurricane Watch	978-1-935053-00-2
Melissa Good	Red Sky At Morning	978-1-932300-80-2
Melissa Good	Storm Surge: Book One	978-1-935053-28-6
Melissa Good	Storm Surge: Book Two	978-1-935053-39-2
Melissa Good	Thicker Than Water	1-932300-24-4
Melissa Good	Terrors of the High Seas	1-932300-45-7
Melissa Good	Tropical Storm	978-1-932300-60-4
Melissa Good	Tropical Convergence	978-1-935053-18-7
Regina A. Hanel	Love Another Day	978-1-935053-44-6
Maya Indigal	Until Soon	978-1-932300-31-4
Lori L. Lake	Different Dress	1-932300-08-2
Lori L. Lake	Ricochet In Time	1-932300-17-1
Lori L. Lake	Like Lovers Do	978-1-935053-66-8
K. E. Lane	And, Playing the Role of Herself	978-1-932300-72-7
Helen Macpherson	Love's Redemption	978-1-935053-04-0
J. Y Morgan	Learning To Trust	978-1-932300-59-8
J. Y. Morgan	Download	978-1-932300-88-8
A. K. Naten	Turning Tides	978-1-932300-47-5
Lynne Norris	One Promise	978-1-932300-92-5
Linda S. North	The Dreamer, Her Angel, and the Stars	978-1-935053-45-3
Paula Offutt	Butch Girls Can Fix Anything	978-1-932300-74-1

Surtees and Dunne	True Colours	978-1-932300-529
Surtees and Dunne	Many Roads to Travel	978-1-932300-55-0
Vicki Stevenson	Family Affairs	978-1-932300-97-0
Vicki Stevenson	Family Values	978-1-932300-89-5
Vicki Stevenson	Family Ties	978-1-935053-03-3
Vicki Stevenson	Certain Personal Matters	978-1-935053-06-4
Cate Swannell	Heart's Passage	978-1-932300-09-3
Cate Swannell	No Ocean Deep	978-1-932300-36-9
Cate Swannell	A Long Time Coming	978-1-61929-062-4

About the Author

Cate Swannell is a journalist and writer who lives on the Gold Coast, on the east coast of Australia. She has two other novels under her belt—*Heart's Passage* and *No Ocean Deep*. She is the online editor of news website goldcoast.com.au and can also be found on Twitter (@obfus_cate), Facebook and Tumblr (impeccablesauce.tumblr.com).

VISIT US ONLINE AT
www.regalcrest.biz

At the Regal Crest Website You'll Find

- The latest news about forthcoming titles and new releases

- Our complete backlist of romance, mystery, thriller, adventure, drama, young adult and non-fiction titles

- Information about your favorite authors

- Current bestsellers

- Media tearsheets to print and take with you when you shop

- Which books are also available as eBooks.

Regal Crest print titles are available from all progressive booksellers including numerous sources online. Our distributors are Bella Distribution and Ingram.